Max Powers
and
Project Gemini

Keith Philips

Max Powers and Project Gemini
Copyright © 2017 Keith Philips

Keith Philips
2509 E. Broad St.
Richmond, VA 23223

http://www.keithphilips.com
kp@keithphilips.com

First Edition - February 24th, 2017

Max Powers and Project Gemini

PROLOGUE

Katherine Powers drove down the dark leafy street wondering what she would tell her husband. It had been hard enough during the past week trying to avoid explaining the schedule that kept her at work so late. And now, to show up with a baby in her arms; would it be too much for even the most gentle and understanding man she'd ever known?

The thought of Tim helped quiet her mind. If anyone could accept this radical new reality, he could. She paused to congratulate herself. Everyone, her friends, and family, even people she barely knew, had disapproved of the match. There was no way, they had said, that she and her Ivy League Ph.D., would be compatible with a blue collar machinist. Some wondered aloud if he had even graduated from high school.

Katherine knew things they didn't. She knew how calm and dependable he was. She knew she could trust him and that his unshakable moral compass would guide not only him, but her, and now this baby as well. She glanced over her shoulder to check on the infant as if a sleeping baby could escape his car seat.

Scientopia was the real problem. Tim would have every right to be suspicious of a child from that amusement park. He had never openly expressed concern about her job as vice president of Hoff Enterprises research and development, but she felt that he had secret reservations. Of course, any decent person would have reservations about such a place if they knew what was going on there. And even though she couldn't save the project, she could save the baby.

She glanced again at the sleeping infant and felt a warm maternal feeling. Early in their marriage, Katherine and Tim had learned that they would never have children of their own. At first, the news had been crushing to them both. Over time that sadness was replaced by the happiness they found in each other.

Katharine wondered if this baby would open old wounds. That thought faded away as she pulled into the driveway and struggled to ease the sleeping bundle from the car seat. How could anyone feel anything but love for this beautiful creature, even if he wasn't the most unique baby in the world? As she lifted him her hand brushed the bandage on the back of his neck. She winced and hoped she hadn't caused him any discomfort. She smiled at her new found protectiveness. The incision at the base of his skull was tiny. She paused and tried to smooth down his wispy brown hair. She realized that she had a lot to learn about being a mother. At least she tried.

Tim opened the front door as she walked up the steps. Katherine could barely see his face with the light pouring out from behind his lanky body. She was glad she didn't have to struggle with the keys while holding the baby, but her stomach clutched at the look on Tim's face. Slowly, his look of surprise changed to a soft smile.

"What do we have here?" Tim asked.

"It's a baby. What do you think?"

Tim pulled back the blanket and looked at the small round face. Katherine held her breath while Tim studied the situation silently. He looked at Katherine, the baby, and back again. Pausing as if to ask a question, he stopped himself and looked intently at Katherine. Slowly a smile broke across his face. "He's beautiful."

"He's ours," said Katherine.

Tim nodded.

"There is a catch."

Tim raised his eyebrows.

"His name is Maximilian."

Tim laughed. "Maximilian? As in 'Max Powers?' Isn't that asking for trouble?"

Katherine beamed and closed the door.

CHAPTER 1

Ordinary would have been a step up for the small two-bedroom house at 530 Oakland Avenue.

It was not always the case of course. Built after World War II, during a time of prosperity and hope for the future, the house had come with the latest amenities such as insulated wiring, indoor plumbing, and fireproof asbestos siding.

But as time moved on and the neighborhood became less fashionable, progress demanded the street at the end of the block become a highway. With the community divided by six lanes of asphalt, it became an inhospitable place for children. Many families moved away. As business diminished, shops either closed up or left for strip malls in the suburbs.

None of that mattered to Max Powers, the twelve-year-old boy who lived there. He had a vague awareness of not being as well off as the other kids at school. Max had never been on a fancy vacation or gone away to summer camp. He knew nothing about the shows on premium cable channels that the other kids talked about.

On the other hand, his classmates had no knowledge of the things that interested Max. Max's father made one concession to luxury, and that was a computer with an Internet connection. It was Max's link to a larger world. Through it, he had developed a curiosity about all things scientific. For hours, he would follow web links on topics that attracted his interest. Lately, he had been learning about game theory. He suspected this was going to be useful to him as a leading player in the online world of Roblox, a gathering place for all of his friends except one.

"Max? Wake up!" Max's father reached through the door and turned off the ceiling fan. As it began to slow, the rockets painted on the end of each blade became clear.

At night, the glowing constellations that Max and his father had painstakingly mapped across the ceiling were visible.

Max bolted upright in his bed. "Am I late?"

"Not yet, what time did you go to sleep?" asked his father.

"I don't remember."

"Were you playing on the computer?"

"For a while. I was teaching sword fighting to some noobs."

"Max, if you can't limit your playing, I'll have to. There's more to life than Roblox."

"OK, Dad."

Max got out of bed and grabbed a pair of shorts and a shirt from his top drawer.

"Max, those don't match," said his father.

Max looked at the blue plaid shorts and striped shirt. "Oh, yeah," he said.

"Don't you think you should wear long pants?"

Max pulled a rumpled pair of trousers out of the drawer. "These are the only ones that fit, and they have a hole."

Holes in his pants didn't usually bother Max, but today it gave him an excuse to wear shorts.

His father took the pants and looked at the hole in the knee. Fortunately, warm weather meant several more months before having to buy new clothes.

"You know you don't have to go," his father said. "You can stay with me; I enjoyed having you around the shop last week."

Ever since winning the physics category at the Chandler Charter School science fair, and a spot in the Scientopia Science Genius summer program, Max had been afraid that his father wouldn't allow him to participate.

"Please, Dad, I really want to go. I may never have a chance like this again!"

Mr. Powers glanced around the room and reached to turn off the rotating Earth-Moon system that served as Max's night-light. He thought about how much simpler life had been when he made the light for four-year-old Max.

"Okay, you can go. But one bit of trouble and I'm coming to bring you home."

"Why don't you like Scientopia, Dad? It's all about science."

"I don't know exactly. There's something unreal about it."

"Oh, Dad."

"Are you going to take that with you?" Mr. Powers asked, pointing to the talisman hanging from Max's neck. "You might lose it."

Max rubbed his fingers across the gold disk, a constant reminder of his mother. "I guess not," said Max.

He had worn it almost every day since his mother died seven years earlier. The ribbon that held the medallion was frayed and dirty. He'd hate to lose it on a ride. He reluctantly removed the necklace and laid it in his desk drawer.

Max finished getting dressed.

"Hurry up Max. The bus is coming," his father called from the living room.

Max scooped up his worn backpack and headed for the door.

Tim grabbed Max's arm to slow him down. He tried flattening the tufts of stringy brown hair standing straight up from Max's head.

"Tie your shoes, Max."

"Don't have time, Dad."

Max ran out to the bus. As it drove off, he looked back at his house and saw his dad watching from the front steps. As Max settled into his seat, he realized that this would be his first night away from home. Max bit his lip and forced a smile.

Hannah plopped down in the seat next to Max and started talking, as she always did. "My mom wouldn't leave me alone this morning. She made me try on three different outfits before picking one. Then she had to iron it and put a bow in my hair. I don't know why she bothers, everything will be a mess by lunch," she said while pulling out the bow holding her ponytail. Hannah's hair exploded in a riot of black curls.

"Whatcha doing, Max?" she asked.

"Shhh, I'm watching this movie," replied Max.

"What do you mean? I don't see anything."

Hannah leaned in front of Max as she looked at the screen on the seat back in front of him. Max tried to pull back from the black mass blocking his view.

"Hannah!" Max said.

"Cool. What is this?" asked Hannah. "Does it have sound?"

Max pushed Hannah's mop of hair out of the way. "Sit down, you have one, too. Put your thumb on this pad."

Hannah pressed her thumb onto the pad built into her armrest. A second later an image appeared on the screen in front of her.

"Can you see this?" she asked. "I don't hear anything."

"You have to be right in front of the screen. Lean back in your seat and you can hear it." Max had paused his video to show Hannah what to do.

"It's like 3D without glasses."

Max stopped himself from rolling his eyes. Hannah was his best friend, and she knew everything about astronomy, and that kind of stuff, but in many things, she was hopeless.

"It's a hologram. Well, they call it a *Hoffogram*, but it's practically the same thing. You don't need glasses. They invented it at Hoff Labs, but I didn't think it had moved past the prototype stage."

"Look, it knows my name!" said Hannah.

The narrator was saying; "Hannah Phan, you have been assigned to Team Ritchie. When you exit the bus, enter through the Ritchie turnstile where you will receive further directions. The whole Scientopia family is pleased to have you as a member of our Science Genius program. We hope you enjoy your summer."

As Hannah glanced at each of the icons on the screen, they lit up and spun. "Sweet!" said Hannah. "It knows which button I'm looking at!"

"What would you like to learn more about, Hannah?" asked the narrator.

"Really? It knows your name?" asked Max as he stretched sideways to look at her screen.

"Hey, watch it," said Hannah.

"That's funny; my video said *Verner Hoff*. Probably a glitch. The programmers must use Mr. Hoff's name as the default," said Max.

"I'm on Team Ritchie, what about you?" asked Hannah.

"Ritchie."

"What is Richie? Like Richie Rich?"

"Not Richie, It's Ritchie - with a *t*. As in Dennis Ritchie," said Max.

"Who's that?"

Max couldn't help rolling his eyes. "Don't you know anything? He's only the most influential computer programmer ever."

"I've never heard of him, he couldn't be that important," said Hannah.

"Whatever."

The hydrogen-fueled bus zoomed silently down the private highway. The smooth ride made it feel like they were traveling much slower than ninety miles per hour. Periodically, the driver would look up from his phone to check the guidance systems and make sure the bus was still on course, then return to his game.

Max and Hannah were so absorbed in the Hoffogram 3D environment they missed the transit through the underground passageway leading into Scientopia. Only when the bus slowed did the passengers take their eyes off their screens.

"Hey look, we're here!" said Hannah.

An attractive woman in her twenties stood waiting for the bus. She was holding up a paddle with a cardboard star, Scientopia's logo. She was wearing a short dress and calf-high boots, the distinctive Scientopia uniform.

"Summer Geniuses, gather around me, please. Children, please be quiet so you can hear."

"That's a stupid looking outfit," Hannah whispered to Max. "It looks like something from the original *Star Trek*."

"I think it's supposed to," said Max.

"It's stupid. If they wanted to steal from bad science fiction they could have at least used the uniforms from *The Next Generation*, they're much more practical," said Hannah.

"What's bad about *Star Trek*? It was the first great science fiction on TV."

"Are you kidding? Walking around like nothing's happening when they jump to warp speed? Have you ever heard of acceleration? They would be smashed like bugs on the back wall."

"Whatever."

"Children, I'm Ms. Barrett, and I'll be your guide today."

"Why is she calling us children?" whispered Hannah. "Doesn't she know we'll be teenagers next year?"

"Shhh."

At that moment, Max noticed Ryan Fairchild stepping off the bus late, as usual.

"Hey Maxie," Ryan said. "What did I miss?"

"Nothing," answered Max.

"Who's the hottie?"

"That's Ms. Barrett, our guide."

"Cool." Ryan ran his fingers through his blonde hair and gave Max a "watch me operate" wink.

"Children, if you will just go through the turnstile labeled with your team name we'll meet on the other side. Does everyone know their team name?"

Ryan approached Ms. Barrett and flashed a grin. "Miss, I'm Ryan Fairchild, and I seem to have missed my team name."

"Yes, Ryan, you're on Team Turing."

"Thanks," said Ryan, with a little wrinkle of his nose.

"Did you see that?" said Hannah. "Does he think she likes him? What is she, like forty?"

"Ms. Barrett, I'm Max Powers on Team Ritchie. I think there's a problem with my ID. The name on my video was Verner Hoff."

"Don't worry about it, sweetie, just go through the turnstile, and we'll get it sorted out later." Ms. Barrett smiled warmly at Max, who blushed.

The kids lined up at the turnstiles and took turns placing their fingers on the biometric fingerprint readers. "Welcome, Hannah Phan," chirped a synthetic voice. "Enjoy your stay at Scientopia." Hannah smiled at Max, who was waiting for his turn to enter the park.

Max put his thumb on the pad. "Welcome, Mr. Hoff," said the voice. Max shook his head, continued through, and joined his group.

"That was weird," Max muttered to himself. "I wonder why I'm not in the system?"

A few miles from Scientopia, an old split-level house, clad in peeling paint, sat surrounded by an unkempt lawn. As unremarkable as the outside was, the inside was less so. In the kitchen, green Formica countertops rested on pine cabinets with the finish long since worn away. The countertops were cluttered with dirty dishes and empty frozen dinner trays.

Upstairs, a hall with hardwood flooring that hadn't been waxed in a decade led to three bedrooms with floors covered by matted shag carpet. In the first bedroom, a mattress and box spring sat on the floor. Next to the bed, a lamp rested on an inverted milk crate. There were piles of dirty clothes scattered around the room.

The second bedroom was empty. Farther down the hall was another that showed more care than any other part of the house. It wasn't the desk – three hollow doors laid on homemade sawhorses – or the high-tech swivel chair that made the room special.

The equipment on the makeshift desk made this space unique – powerful computers usually available only to the military or government intelligence agencies. They hummed along day and night, monitoring news sources and databases throughout the world. The equipment generated so much heat the central air conditioning system couldn't keep up. A large window unit made up the difference.

A DS3 line, connected to a router the size of a refrigerator, provided an almost endless stream of data to the system – more information than the data carrying capacity of a small city. Much of this information was being accessed illegally from the most exclusive and expensive databases on the planet. The system's owner,

Sergey Mamontov, felt the world owed him something. Data was payment enough, at least for now.

A message arrived from a forgotten subsystem at Hoff Labs, triggering an alert on the far right-hand monitor. Mamontov clicked to open and read the message. He paused, took a deep breath, and scanned the message again to make sure he had read it right. Slowly a grin spread across his face. The person he'd been looking for all these years had finally come to him.

CHAPTER 2

The Crystal Tower was the centerpiece of Scientopia. The glory of the Crystal Tower wasn't its size or height but the thousands of OLED panels that covered its exterior. They could make the tower look like anything from a castle to a mirror to a striped piece of candy. From a distance, the Crystal Tower looked *big*. On closer inspection, the Crystal Tower was *immense*.

As Ms. Barrett and the Summer Geniuses approached the Crystal Tower, a short, blonde boy pointed up and exclaimed, "Hey, look at that!"

The star at the pinnacle of the Crystal Tower was changing colors and rotating slowly.

"Does it always do that, Ms. Barrett?" the blonde boy asked.

"No. I've never seen it do that. Before Scientopia's founder, Mr. Hoff, died it was only supposed to do that when he was in the park."

Floating in the center of the Crystal Tower's thirty-story atrium, suspended by six carbon fiber cables, was a transparent sphere that gave the distinct impression of the Death Star. OLED panels covered the sphere, but most of the time they were left clear so that visitors could catch a glimpse of the inner workings of Hoff Labs. Entering the atrium, the Summer Geniuses couldn't avoid being impressed, even those who had visited the park before.

"We're going up into that?" asked Hannah pointing to the gigantic ball.

"That's right," said Ms. Barrett. "Hoff Labs is located inside the Orb. It's where you'll be spending your summer."

Max was amazed by the Crystal Tower and the Orb. He could see why the Orb reminded people of the Death

Star, even though at the moment, it was mirrored and flashing like a rotating disco ball.

"How do they make it move?" asked a tall girl with red hair.

Ms. Barrett smiled. "It's not moving. Like the outside of the Crystal Tower, the Orb is covered with OLED panels. The images on the panels make it look like it's in motion. Watch, it's about to change. See, there it is, a rolling eight ball."

As the show ended the screens went clear, and scientists were visible at work in their labs. Ms. Barrett led the group to the elevator directly beneath the Orb.

The elevator was completely transparent. Not like those elevators in malls and hotels that were a combination of metal and glass. It was constructed entirely of a see-through polycarbonate polymer. To observers on the ground, it looked as if people were pulled into the Orb by an invisible tractor beam. When the lights were on, the shaft glowed, making passengers look like they were riding a beam of light.

As they ascended, Max pulled back from the edge. He looked down at his feet and saw the atrium far below. He placed his hand against the side of the car to steady himself.

Ryan noticed and leaned closer to whisper in Max's ear. "What's the matter Maxie, afraid you're going to fall?" He gave Max a little shove towards the edge. Max replied with a nasty look but did nothing else.

Ms. Barrett continued her explanation of the elevator technology. "The car is raised and lowered with air pressure like the tubes you may have seen at a bank drive-through. We couldn't get safety approval to use air alone. The glass cables you see overhead are there as a backup system. Our biggest problem as far as visibility is the fingerprints people put on the inside and the scuff marks on the floor. That's why you feel that sponginess under your feet. It's a gel mat that protects the floor."

The elevator rose into the Orb and continued to ascend. "We're going to Level Zero," said Ms. Barrett. "It's at the equator of the Orb. Levels above the equator have labels with positive numbers. Those below with negative numbers. On each level rooms are labeled by rings starting with 'A' in the center. As you move clockwise around the ring individual room numbers will increase. For example, 0A1 is the lecture hall located right in the center of the Orb. It's where you will have most of your group classes."

As they exited the elevator, Hannah whispered to Max, "Why do you let him do that to you?"

Max tried to act ignorant.

"I saw Ryan shove you. Don't let him push you around like that," said Hannah.

Max lowered his head and muttered, "I'm just a geek. It's what we do."

"Don't be stupid. Everyone here is a geek."

Max looked at Hannah and brightened. It was the first time the idea had occurred to him. "Yeah, I guess you're right," he said. "Ryan's just so confident. I don't know how he does it."

"My mom says too much confidence is used to hide fear."

Like the other rooms in the Orb, the pie-shaped amphitheater had glass walls. The narrow end of the room, where the speaker stood, was nestled against the elevator. When the screen wasn't turned on you could see through to watch people going up and down, which was welcome entertainment when the speaker was boring. Unfortunately for the Summer Geniuses, experience had taught the instructors to turn on the screen and darken the walls. At least some of the instructors were kind enough to provide interesting images on the inside.

"Hey Maxie, move over so I can sit next to Neil," said Ryan.

Max looked up at Ryan and wondered how a twelve-year-old could be so tall and confident. It was annoying.

"Why don't you sit somewhere else hair boy?" sneered Hannah.

Ryan stroked his perfect blonde hair. "Look, Maxie, your girlfriend is sticking up for you. Does she cut your meat too?" Ryan elbowed his friend, Neil Singh, and they both laughed. "Now move."

"Only if you ask nicely," said Max.

"Will you move, pleeease?"

Max recognized the mockery in Ryan's tone, but he thought the point had been made and moved to the seat on the other side of Hannah.

"Children, if you will all be quiet and take your seats, Steve will be here shortly," said Ms. Barrett.

The announcement had the opposite of its intended effect. The students buzzed louder at the prospect of seeing the world-famous Steve Hunter. Some of them found places in the theater-style seats, but others remained standing.

Ms. Barrett once again said, "Children, Steve is on his way in; please take your seats."

The room erupted into applause as Steve stepped into the stage lights. Wearing his trademark olive green t-shirt, faded jeans, and sandals, he walked casually to the center of the stage and stood, accepting the adoration of the Summer Geniuses. After a few moments, he raised his hand. "Thank you," his voice boomed over the sound system.

As the applause subsided he said, "Thank you, but I should be applauding you, the newest members of the most selective, the most prestigious, the most advanced youth science camp in the galaxy, the Scientopia Science

Genius program." Steve started clapping, and the room went wild with cheers.

He smiled and waited for the audience to calm down. "We are so proud to have you, our best class ever. This year our Geniuses come from twenty different states. Among your group seventeen have completed advanced placement exams, three have earned perfect SAT scores, two have published papers in major peer-reviewed scientific journals, and one is a Junior Olympian. Do you know what the best part is? No one is older than fourteen."

The room exploded with another round of clapping and cheering.

Steve grinned, looked at the floor, shook his head, and said, "I wish I had been as smart and motivated when I was your age. With a start like this, there's nothing you can't accomplish."

Steve paused and scanned the audience. Max wasn't certain, but he thought that Steve's gaze rested for a bit too long on him.

"This summer it doesn't matter what you have or haven't done in the past. You're here to set the world of Scientopia on fire! You will be working with some of the best scientists in the world on emerging technologies developed here at Scientopia. Our experts in robotics, communications, programming, materials, and other disciplines will help you develop new ways to solve a great challenge for Scientopia and the rest of humanity."

Steve snapped his fingers, and the room went dark. A video appeared on the huge screen behind the stage. It showed a photo of a smiling young Verner Hoff and Steve Hunter in lab coats. A narrator with a warm baritone spoke.

"Scientopia is the realization of a vision shared by scientist-entrepreneur Verner Hoff and creative genius Steve Hunter. Conceived as a way to solve tomorrow's problems today and excite people about the possibilities of the future, Scientopia is part theme park, part research lab, part government contractor, and part responsible corporate citizen."

"Hoff Labs is at the forefront of developing technologies, such as artificial intelligence, data mining, sensors, and robotics. Many Fortune 500 companies and numerous governments around the world use technologies developed and licensed by Hoff Enterprises. Hoff Enterprises. . ."

The video went on for several minutes detailing the accomplishments of Hoff Enterprises. When the lights came back up, Steve was standing to the side of the stage. "Is that exciting or what? We have a few minutes before your behind-the-scenes tour of Scientopia, so I'll take a few questions."

Steve picked up a pair of glasses from the podium and slipped them on. "OK, who's first?"

Steve pointed at a cute brunette. "Sabrina, what's your question?"

The girl stood and asked, "How did you know my name? I was going to ask if it's true you're a vegan?"

Steve broke into a huge smile. "Yes, I am a vegan. And I know your name, Sabrina Fogel, through the miracle of augmented reality." Steve pointed at his glasses, and then to the screen behind him, and immediately the screen mirrored what Steve was seeing. As he looked into the audience, a computer-generated tag popped up showing the name of whoever he was looking at. Once the kids realized what they were seeing, ooh's and aah's rippled through the auditorium.

"Pretty sick, right?" said Steve. "How do you think these work? Tommy Pace?"

"There's someone in the back typing in the names," replied Tommy.

"That would work for a small group, but we're already testing this on everyone who visits the park. How might we do that? Merrick Garner?"

"RFID chips?"

"Radio Frequency ID chips is a good guess, but not what we're using. What do you think Max Powers?"

Max was startled. His hand wasn't up. "Facial recognition?"

"That's right! Gold star for Max. What do you think is our biggest hurdle using this approach?"

Max rolled his eyes upwards in thought. "It would be the time it takes to get a match from the database."

"Any ideas, Max, on how we might solve this problem?"

"If you limited the search to people you knew were in the park, and the glasses were always actively scanning they would be ready with the identification when you asked for it."

Steve spread his arms in amused astonishment. "It looks like we've identified our first real genius. That's exactly right Max."

"How did you know that?" whispered Hannah once Steve had moved on to other questions.

Max shrugged.

As Steve was leaving the stage, he turned to his assistant. "Find out everything you can about Max Powers."

Ten minutes later Dr. Dieter Lehrer walked to the front of the amphitheater. He was big, powerful, and physically perfect. His blonde hair was cut short, showing his chiseled features. One look and you knew he was someone who didn't put up with nonsense.

He stood without speaking and looked coldly from side to side. Without a word the Summer Geniuses took their seats, and silence fell over the room.

"Ladies and gentlemen, that took entirely too long. When I enter the room, you will immediately take your seats and be silent."

Dr. Lehrer's German accent was thick but no one had any trouble understanding his instructions. The students sat rigidly. No one wanted to become the focus of his steely gaze.

"We will now bid farewell to the lovely Ms. Barrett and thank her for her services. She will return to her duties in public relations and leave you in my charge. For the next eight weeks, you belong to me. You will learn more than you ever thought possible. You will get to do things that people twice your age have not experienced. It will be difficult, but also rewarding."

Ryan leaned over to Neil Singh and whispered, "This sounds like fun."

Neil giggled.

Dr. Lehrer glared at the pair. "Mr. Fairchild, do you have something to say? Could you share the joke?"

Ryan flushed red. "No. No, sir."

Dr. Lehrer continued. "You are not here to have fun. You are here to learn and contribute. Despite that, you will have fun because the ideas and technologies we work with are so exciting. The things we create here to amuse and educate the guests at Scientopia will be further developed to make people's lives better. If you think that is fun, then you are in the right place. If you think fun has anything to do with games or silliness, then I think you would be happier spending your summer elsewhere. Is there anyone who would like to leave?"

No one moved or spoke and most held their breath.

"Very well then," said Dr. Lehrer, his manner visibly softened. "Now I have the pleasure of introducing your caretaker for the summer."

"Alistair, will you please come in?"

A door at the back of the stage opened, and a five-foot tall android entered. The class buzzed with excitement. Every kid in the country knew the beloved Alistair. Meeting him seemed too good to be true.

Alistair removed his top hat and bowed, revealing a bald head trimmed with tufts of gray hair on either side. He looked around the room with a cheerful smile that crinkled the pink skin around his wide, sparkling eyes.

"You honor me too much," Alistair said. He took a handkerchief from his old-fashioned jacket and wiped an imaginary tear from his chubby cheek.

"Do you have a Hoffpop Alistair?" someone shouted from the far side of the room.

"Oh dear!" said Alistair as he fumbled in the pockets of the red waistcoat that covered his round belly. "I'm afraid I don't have enough for everyone; do you mind sharing?"

The class laughed.

"That will be enough," said Dr. Lehrer. "I see you already know the famous Alistair T. Pfefferbottom. Despite his whimsical appearance, Alistair is the most advanced android on the planet and one of the biggest attractions in Scientopia. We call all our robotic friends *ani-droids*, for animated androids, because they are so much more lifelike than a typical robot. For many guests, Alistair is the highlight of their visit. Usually, his primary duty is greeting guests, but this summer we are working on upgrades and system maintenance. We decided that an excellent way to test our progress would be to have him serve as your guide. What would you like to say to the class Alistair?"

"Welcome to Scientopia, Summer Geniuses. Please let me know if you need any assistance, and I will help you in any way possible," said Alistair.

"Children, we have a problem with Alistair," said Dr. Lehrer.

"Only one?" quipped Alistair.

The class laughed, and Dr. Lehrer displayed his first smile, saying "Yes, well, only one that we will admit to. You see Alistair is one of a kind. Does anyone know why?"

The class was silent for a moment. Then Max spoke up. "The optical chip?"

"Yes Mr. Powers, how did you know that?"

Max shrugged. "It just came to me."

"The optical chip Mr. Powers is referring to was created by my friend Verner Hoff. Very few know about this chip." Dr. Lehrer stared intently at Max, who slid down in his seat to make himself less conspicuous.

Dr. Lehrer continued. "The chip's computing power, combined with Mr. Hoff's integrated program design has made Alistair the most intelligent of any artificial device in existence."

Max thought he saw Alistair flash a look of indignation when Dr. Lehrer referred to him as a device. *That's some sophisticated programming*, thought Max.

"When Mr. Hoff passed away a dozen years ago, all knowledge of the chip's design and creation died with him. We have not been able to replicate his success. Perhaps the work we will do this summer will allow us to learn Alistair's secrets so that we can make more ani-droids like him."

Dr. Lehrer smiled. "Who knows? Maybe one of you will unlock Alistair's secrets."

"You will each be assigned to teams that will contribute to this year's project. It is crucial to Hoff Labs and the park that we duplicate Verner Hoff's work. We need ani-droids to cover more locations around the park. Finally, should something happen to Alistair, we need a replacement."

Alistair displayed an expression of concern. The audience laughed.

"I'm sorry Alistair," said Dr. Lehrer, "we certainly don't plan on letting anything happen to you."

As he continued, Dr. Lehrer began to pace slowly around the room. "You have been selected and placed into teams with this very project in mind. I hope that your young minds will bring fresh ideas so that we may make progress."

Dr. Lehrer stopped abruptly and turned to face the class. "What makes this project so very exciting is that it will be a practical exercise. You will have access to the components used to construct Alistair, and it will be up to each team to put them together in a way that is as good or better than our artificial friend."

Alistair, once again, seemed disturbed by Dr. Lehrer's remarks.

"As you can see," said Dr. Lehrer, "Alistair displays reactions that appear to be human. If we could understand how he does that and what it means, it would be a great stride forward not only for robotics but artificial intelligence in general."

"Alistair, display teams."

On the screen behind the doctor, the team rosters appeared, each with four members.

"You will see that each team has members from the specialties of mechanics, materials, electronics, and programming. Team captains are indicated by an asterisk."

Max found his name under Team Ritchie. There was an asterisk beside it. He felt a wave of nervousness wash over him that came close to nausea.

Hannah was pulling his arm frantically. "Max, you're the team captain!"

Max barely heard her. All he could think about was the responsibility of being team captain. He didn't want to be in charge. He wished he could just disappear.

"Hey, Maxie!"

It was Ryan speaking from several chairs away. "Get ready to be crushed, little man."

Max looked at the screen again and found Ryan's name, listed under Team Turing, with an asterisk right beside it.

CHAPTER 3

Max heard Hannah saying something: "Max, Max, are you listening to me?"

Max looked around and realized that he was in the food court in the Crystal Tower atrium. He had been lost in thought since discovering he was Team Ritchie's captain.

"Isn't it great," Hannah was saying, "being on the same team, and you as captain? I have some ideas about the project that we can discuss later."

"I don't want to be team captain!" Max whispered to himself not intending for Hannah to hear.

"Why wouldn't you want to be team captain? You are so lucky! I wish I had been picked," said Hannah.

"Wanna trade?" asked Max.

Hannah wrinkled her brow and pursed her lips in thought. "I don't think we can do that. You shouldn't want to anyway. You're really good at listening to people. And, it's an honor to be team captain."

Max pushed the orange chicken around on his plate. He must have followed Hannah through the food line. He didn't even like Chinese. "What about Ryan?"

"What about Ryan?" Hannah asked.

"He's the Team Turing captain, and he has it in for me."

"Don't be ridiculous. Remember, he's just a geek, too. We're going to destroy him!"

After lunch, the kids were subjected to a parade of scientists droning on about their specialties and how vital they were to the project. Max fought to stay awake. He decided that he shouldn't have loaded up on so much cake after throwing out the orange chicken. Having so many dishes to choose from was a new experience for him. His dad usually sent him to school with a bag lunch. At Scientopia, the menu was virtually endless.

Max heard an unfamiliar adult voice.

"All right geniuses, are we ready to have some fun? My name is Dr. Greg Symonds. You can call me Greg. I'm the lead engineer for control systems."

An after-lunch stupor had overtaken the group. Greg received a tepid response. He pushed a lock of thin hair from his face and smiled broadly.

"Too much lunch? Do they have you on the unlimited plan?"

A few of the kids nodded.

"That'll do it. I'll tell you a little secret. Don't miss the hamburgers and shakes at the Galaxy Grill. The best desserts are in the Computer Café, but I would stay away from the Silicon Chip Pie. Get the Hi-Res Root Beer float instead."

"This afternoon you get to play with some of the coolest toys you've ever seen!" Greg continued.

Max and several other kids sat up and began to listen.

"These helmets, for example," said Greg as he motioned to a table, "create the most advanced integration between your brain, the physical world, and the world of data that is currently possible. Some people call it augmented reality, but I prefer to think of it as a different reality we haven't been able to access until very recently."

He picked up a helmet, which looked something like a fighter pilot's helmet with a visor. A box with a small antenna was attached to the back.

"This is an advanced version of the glasses you may have seen around the park. I think Steve was wearing a pair for his talk this morning. The difference is how much data these can tap into as well as the ability for them to interact with your brain waves. These helmets have access to most of the computer systems and databases here at Scientopia, but we've found that it takes a good deal of practice for anyone to use the interface effectively. It's extremely difficult to control anything using only brain waves. Perhaps one of you will surprise us and be able to move something on the screen. Who wants to be first?"

No one volunteered.

"No need to be scared," said Greg, "it's perfectly safe."

Several hands shot up. "OK, Ryan, why don't you start us off?"

Ryan put on the helmet. Greg tapped some controls on his tablet, and what Ryan saw appeared on the screen at the front of the room.

"You can see that the helmet is identifying everyone, and Ryan sees your names displayed above your heads. OK, Ryan, try to open the folder next to Hannah's name?

"I can't move it," said Ryan.

"You're doing fine," said Greg. "Try slowing down and relaxing. The helmet can detect stress."

Ryan took a deep breath. The cursor indicating Ryan's visual focus moved closer to the folder.

"That's great," said Greg. "Blink and see if you can open the folder."

Ryan blinked, and the folder sprang open. Text appeared in a box over Hannah's head.

"Excellent. I've never seen anyone do it on the first try before. The text you see is a log file showing Hannah's interaction with the park today. At the top was the last thing she did, which was to enter this classroom. You can see where she took the elevator into the Orb and before that she had orange chicken for lunch. Good job, Ryan. Who wants to go next?"

Max watched as the others tried the helmet, with varying degrees of success.

"Is there anyone who hasn't gone yet?" asked Greg.

Max half raised his hand.

"OK, Max, come down here, and give it a shot."

Max walk slowly to the front of the class, picked the helmet up and placed it on his head.

"Ready?" asked Greg.

Max nodded.

As the display flickered to life, Max saw Steve and the other kids, each with a virtual name tag floating above their heads. He then heard a voice that said: "Welcome Mr. Hoff, where would you like to go?"

"It's asking where I would like to go. What should I say?" asked Max. No one had mentioned hearing a voice, and he didn't know what to do.

"No one said anything, Max. Choose a member of the group and try to open their folder," said Greg.

Max hesitated. He suddenly had felt an urge to see the view from the top of the Crystal Tower. The helmet display and the overhead screen instantly flashed to a birds-eye view of Scientopia.

"What are you doing Max? How did you do that?" asked Greg.

"I don't know!" Maxed blurted nervously.

Max had no idea how he had done it. His fear of heights took over and he wished he was much closer to the ground. Instantly, the display shifted to a view of what looked like an underground access tunnel.

"Max, come back to the classroom please," said Greg.

The image on Max's visor returned to the classroom. It was getting a little harder to focus; Max had begun to hear a faint buzzing inside his head. He had a bizarre feeling that he was somehow in communication with the whole park, all at the same time.

"Max, see if you can access one of your classmates' folders," Greg suggested.

Max looked at Ryan's folder. It opened immediately and displayed the same kind of information that had come up for Hannah. Inside Max's head, however, a familiar voice told him much more about Ryan - his parents' names, his address, all the schools he had attended, his grades, even the sites he had visited online. There was so much data that Max couldn't focus on any single thing.

"Very good," said Greg. "We have two geniuses who seem to have exceptional abilities with the helmet, so let's play a little game."

"Ryan, you put on the other helmet, and I'm going to put you both in a combat simulation. You will be Darth Vader and Luke Skywalker battling it out with lightsabers. The trick is to move the avatars with your minds. Moving your hands or bodies won't do any good. Ryan, who do you want to be?"

Ryan smiled underneath the helmet. "Vader."

"OK, Max, you're Luke Skywalker. When the simulation begins you both need to figure out how to activate your lightsabers. Remember, you must do this with your mind."

An image appeared on Max's display. It was a first-person perspective. There was a lightsaber hilt in his right hand. Vader stood directly in front of him, two steps away.

Max was *home*. This was like Roblox on steroids! He shifted instantly into combat mode. *On*, he thought.

A green plasma blade sprang into existence. Next, he visualized himself lunging forward and slicing off Vader's head.

Before he realized what had happened, the class erupted like a soccer stadium after a winning goal. Apparently, he had won.

Max heard Ryan's voice, "That's not fair, I wasn't ready."

The simulation vanished.

"Let's try that again," said Greg. "Max, this time wait until Ryan has his lightsaber on before starting."

Max nodded. He was becoming increasingly distracted by the buzz inside his head. It kept getting louder.

The simulation restarted, and Max saw the Vader avatar standing where it had been before. Max remained motionless. Vader began to move and after a few seconds a red plasma blade appeared. Max left his lightsaber off. He watched as Vader waved his plasma blade awkwardly in the air before aiming at Max's torso.

Instinctively Max thought: *jump*. His avatar leaped several feet straight up. A moment later, as Max's feet hit the floor, it was clear that Vader's guard was down. He sprang forward and used his lightsaber hilt as a club, knocking Vader's weapon to the floor and Vader to his knees.

Darth Vader cowered beneath Max's pitiless gaze.

Max activated his plasma blade. In a single fluid motion, he cut Vader in half, head to toe.

Max expected to hear his classmates at that moment, but the buzzing in his head now blocked all other sounds. It had become too intense. Random images from Scientopia flooded his brain. Without knowing why, he shouted, "Project Gemini!"

Max collapsed to the floor. The buzzing in his head stopped, and everything went quiet. The last thing he heard before losing consciousness was Hannah yelling, "Max!"

CHAPTER 4

Max's eyelids were too heavy to open. He heard familiar voices, but couldn't identify them.

"The doctors say he will be all right. They can't find anything wrong with him."

Another voice said, "What happened, was it the helmet?"

"The helmet shouldn't be able to cause anything like that."

There was a pause and the first voice continued, "There was one thing, though. In the few minutes he had the helmet on, it downloaded sixty terabytes of data. That's at least a hundred times the average transfer rate."

"Do you know why?"

There was no response.

Slowly, Max forced his eyes open just enough to take in his surroundings. He was in a hospital bed with monitoring equipment on either side. He saw Greg and Steve leaving the room.

Steve said, "We need to keep an eye on him."

Max didn't think Steve was talking about his medical condition.

The next time Max woke up he heard a girl's voice whispering his name. As he opened his eyes, he saw Hannah sitting in a chair next to the bed with a concerned expression on her face.

"Hey, how're you doing?" Hannah asked.

Max's throat and mouth were dry. It was difficult to speak. He managed a whisper, "Water." Hannah poured water into a plastic cup from a small plastic pitcher.

After a few sips, he asked, "What happened?"

"It was the weirdest thing," said Hannah. "After you destroyed Ryan's avatar everyone was cheering, and you just collapsed on the floor."

Max hesitated. Should he tell Hannah what he remembered? He wasn't sure he should tell anyone. It was all so hazy and unreal. They would probably think he was crazy.

Before he could decide what to say, Hannah asked, "What's Project Gemini?"

For some reason this annoyed Max. Sometimes Hannah asked silly questions.

"Duh, the constellation with the twins."

"I don't think so," said Hannah.

Max froze. He was flooded with a new set of memories. He felt fear creeping over his body.

"What is it, Max?"

He shook his head. "Nothing."

Hannah looked at him as he tried to avoid her gaze. "It doesn't seem like nothing."

Max was silent. He didn't know what to say to Hannah. She wasn't going to leave this alone.

"Are you going to be all right?" Hannah asked.

He didn't want to lie to her. "I don't know."

"What happened? You can tell me; I can keep a secret."

Max didn't know if she *could* keep a secret, but she was his best friend, and he realized that it was too much to keep to himself.

"I saw things."

"What things?"

Max paused for a second and then continued. "Everything going on in the park."

"Everything?" Hannah asked.

"Everything. I could see data on the number of visitors in the park, the location of everyone with a tracking beacon, the status of every ride, the view from every camera. I could even see through Alistair's eyes."

"Could you read my mind?" asked Hannah nervously.

"No. Just the machines. The computers." Max paused for a second and thought. "I did know almost anything about everyone, though. Where they live, what their job is, even what websites they visit."

"How much do you remember?

Max nodded. "All of it."

Max heard footsteps and a familiar voice. "Hi, kids!"

It was Mr. Powers. Max wondered if his dad had been standing there long.

"How are you doing, buddy?" his dad asked as he moved to Max's bedside.

"I'm fine, Dad."

"I brought you a Reece's Cup." Mr. Powers handed Max the candy, his favorite. "Quite a first day at camp wasn't it?"

Max nodded and busied himself with opening the Reece's two-pack. He handed Hannah one and took a bite from the other. Max felt better already. He smiled weakly and wondered how much his father had heard.

"What about you Hannah? I hope your day wasn't as exciting as Max's."

"No, Mr. Powers. Well, I should get going, I have to get back to the team. We have a class after dinner."

When Hannah was gone, Max's Dad sat in the chair next to his bed and said nothing.

After what seemed to Max like a hundred years, Mr. Powers finally spoke, "Are you ready to come home? I don't think this is the place for you."

Max didn't know what to say. He *did* want to go home. He didn't want to be team leader, and he didn't want to deal with Ryan. Most of all, he wasn't sure he wanted to know what had happened when he put on the virtual reality helmet. He was scared. He missed his room. He missed playing Roblox with his friends.

"Dad, there's something about this place. It knows me, and I know it. I have to find out why."

Sergey Mamontov pushed back from his keyboard and finished his formerly frozen burrito. He tossed the wrapper towards the trash can and missed.

He couldn't be *sure* what had happened, but Maximilian's medical data combined with the data spike recorded for the virtual reality helmet painted a clear picture.

This was almost certainly the confirmation he had been waiting for. Even so, he couldn't depend solely on data stolen from Hoff Labs networks. He needed to see for himself.

Direct contact posed certain problems. Long ago he had been banned from Scientopia and the facial recognition system ensured that returning wouldn't be easy. Even if he could get in, the infirmary had several more layers of security. It was unlikely that he would make it as far as Maximilian's room.

Sergey noticed an alert on the screen indicating Maximilian's medical chart being updated. The boy would be released in the morning. *This may be possible*, he thought.

Sergey pulled up a browser and Googled "defeat facial recognition." What he found seemed simple enough. He walked to the kitchen to find a nine-volt battery. A trip to the dollar store for some LED flashlights and a bit of electrical tape, and he'd have everything he needed.

The gold paint on Sergey's ancient Chrysler minivan was peeling and flaking. Like his house, the floor of the van was covered with empty wrappers and random pieces of paper. As he got into the decrepit vehicle, his gaze lingered on the house. It was such an embarrassment, considering who he had once been.

He felt things were about to change. He was going to regain what was rightfully his.

CHAPTER 5

Mr. Powers had reluctantly agreed to let Max stay at Scientopia and he was more than ready to leave the infirmary by the time Alistair appeared the next morning. Max knew Alistair was a machine, but when the droid asked him how he was feeling, he seemed so human.

"I guess I made a mess of things, didn't I?" Max asked Alistair as they walked to the Orb.

"It was no inconvenience at all. Guest safety is our number one priority," replied Alistair.

"It was strange," said Max, "seeing everything going on in the park."

Alistair said nothing.

"Do you see everything going on in the park?" asked Max.

Alistair looked at Max and said, "I do not know what you mean."

"Can you see what all the cameras see? Like the one on top of the Crystal Tower."

"I can see only through my own cameras. Can you see through other cameras?"

"I could yesterday when I had the helmet on," replied Max.

"Could you see through my cameras?" asked Alistair.

"Yes."

"Can you now?"

"No. Only when I have the helmet on. But I can remember everything I saw and learned," said Max.

"Is this typical human behavior?" asked Alistair.

"I don't think so."

"Then you are unique."

"So are you Alistair."

Max was nervous as he entered the classroom. He didn't know how the other kids would react to what happened yesterday. He didn't have to wait long to find out. Jimmy McLean and Aiden Fox came up and congratulated him on slicing Ryan to pieces. Lilly Jordan didn't say a word, but she stared at Max with evident admiration.

Dr. Stan Morgan, the software instructor, was describing Alistair's speech recognition algorithms in a glacial monotone. Within minutes, most of the class was nodding off, doodling, or trying to find something to occupy their attention.

Max began sifting through the images he recalled from yesterday's session with the virtual reality helmet. Soon it became clear that what was in his head was a snapshot of the park during the few seconds he was wearing the helmet. Some of the data, such as the status of rides, was useless. Maps and other technical data, however, might come in handy.

Sadly, the information he had retained wasn't organized. It was like having a library in his head, but no catalog to find anything.

Max's attention returned to Dr. Morgan's expressionless voice when he heard him say that Alistair's abilities were limited because he wasn't programmed with true artificial intelligence.

"That's not true," Max muttered under his breath.

"Do you have something to say Mr. Powers?"

Max looked up and before he could stop himself he blurted out, "Alistair does possess artificial intelligence."

"Mr. Powers tell us how that is so, since his operating instructions are compiled in C++?"

"Alistair is programmed in C++, but he has an AI module in Prolog," Max said.

"Mr. Powers I have been through every line of Alistair's programming and assure you, there is no hook to activate a Prolog module."

"It's not activated in the C++. It's in machine language on the communications bus."

Morgan smiled. "And where is the processor to run this program?"

Max looked up and said softly: "It's not a physical chip. It's a virtual machine running inside of the main optical processor."

Morgan looked stricken. It had been his job to reverse engineer Alistair's software systems. He knew more about Alistair's software than anyone. "That's impossible. You can't partition an optical chip."

Max shrugged.

Dr. Morgan was agitated. "Alistair, do you have artificial intelligence capabilities?"

"I do not," replied Alistair.

Dr. Morgan smiled smugly and said, "Don't be concerned Mr. Powers. I've spent years studying Alistair. You couldn't possibly know as much about him as I do."

Max looked at Alistair and said, "Alistair, activate your AI module."

"Please provide authorization code," Alistair's said in a distant monotone.

Max nervously looked at Dr. Morgan, who glared with contempt and amazement.

"Uh," stuttered Max, "36850?"

"AI module activated," said Alistair. Alistair blinked and looked around the room as if he had just awoken from a trance. He scanned all the faces staring silently at him.

"Alistair, do you have artificial intelligence capabilities?" asked Max.

"Yes," responded Alistair.

There were giggles in the class. Max saw several kids smiling at him. Hannah punched him in the arm.

Dr. Morgan's face turned red, and he gave Max a vicious look. "Class come to order! I'm not sure how Mr. Powers managed that little trick, but I'm in no mood for practical jokes. Pay attention; we have a lot to cover." He resumed his droning presentation. Max couldn't understand how he knew so much about Alistair.

It was a huge relief when Dr. Morgan's presentation ended. The entire class was bored and restless, waiting to be released for lunch when Dr. Lehrer entered.

Dr. Lehrer waited until he had everyone's attention and said, "Scholars, I hope you enjoyed Dr. Morgan's lesson on Alistair this morning. Now, I know that you were looking forward to Dr. Weinstein's lecture on Alistair's mechanical systems this afternoon. Unfortunately, he will not be able to be here. Instead, we are going to give you the afternoon to explore the park. Your badges will give you unlimited access to any attraction. Please enjoy yourself, but also pay attention to the science and engineering behind the rides, it will help you with your projects."

Dr. Lehrer paused and then added, "One more thing. Your food cards are unlimited. However, we noticed that there were too many candies and desserts being purchased." Dr. Lehrer tapped a button on his tablet, and a list of food purchases appeared on the wall behind him.

"Please eat responsibly, or we may have to make revisions to your meal plans. You are dismissed."

"Where do you want to go for lunch, Max?" asked Hannah. Without waiting for a response, she continued: "I think we should try the Galaxy Grill. My mom won't let me have milkshakes, and I'm dying to try one. What do you say?"

"OK," said Max.

As they were zipping up their backpacks, Jimmy McLean came up to Max and Hannah. He flashed a freckled grin. "You were awesome, Max," said Jimmy with an enthusiasm that matched his curly red hair. "How did you learn so much about Alistair?"

"It just comes to me," said Max.

"We have the coolest team. I can't wait to get started on the project."

"Me too. What's your specialty?" asked Max.

"Mechanical engineering. My robots have won three championships. I'm bummed we won't get the lecture this afternoon. Where you going to lunch?"

Hannah spoke up. "We're going to the Galaxy Grill to try the milkshakes. Want to come?"

"Nah, I'm lactose intolerant. Aiden wants to try the pizza at Pythagorean Pies, and they've got a soy cheese option. I think I'll go with him. Want to meet up after lunch?"

"Sure," said Max.

"I'll text you."

As Max and Hannah hopped on an Automated Personal Transporter, or APT, Kaylee Johnson heard the music begin. She had six minutes to transform herself from Kaylee Johnson, disgruntled daughter, into Kaylee: beautiful, happy, perky teen star.

Kaylee's mother tried to straighten her daughter's long blonde hair.

"Mom, please. I can do this myself. I've done it a thousand times."

Kaylee had plenty of experience preparing for pageants, shows, and auditions. She had been doing it since she was three years old.

"Kaylee, sometimes I don't think you appreciate me," said her mother. "I'm just trying to help, darling. I want everything to be perfect for my little star."

Mrs. Johnson always said she was just there to encourage Kaylee. To Kaylee, it felt like something else, especially since she started headlining at Scientopia the year before. Three shows a day, six days a week? It was too much work and too much togetherness.

Kaylee wondered what it would be like to have a more normal life. What would it be like to have friends? She was surrounded by people, but they were almost always older. The only people she knew that were her age were a few of the backup dancers and singers in the show. They felt more like employees or competitors than friends. Her mother said they were all jealous and wanted Kaylee's job.

As Kaylee left her dressing room, she sighed and put on her best professional smile.

Hannah slurped the last few drops of her pistachio milkshake and pushed the empty glass toward the middle of the table. "OMG, I'm so stuffed. I can't believe my mom won't let me have milkshakes. They're so good."

Max and Hannah had decided to share three shakes to sample different flavors. Max felt pretty sure she had gotten the biggest part of each one.

"Which one did you like best?" Hannah asked. "I *love* the caramel cappuccino! I'm going to get another one of those."

Max didn't answer. He didn't think she expected him to.

"Ready to ride the Black Hole?" asked Max. "I can't wait!"

Hannah made a disapproving face. "I'm not feeling so good, let's go sit on the bench outside and rest awhile."

Sitting on a bench all afternoon was not what Max had in mind. He had waited too long to visit Scientopia to have his first free afternoon derailed by his milkshake-stuffed best friend. He needed an escape route.

"OK," said Max. "I'll text Jimmy and see if he can meet us at the Black Hole later."

Max followed Hannah to an empty bench, sat down and pulled out his Scientopia-issued phone and started thumbing a message to Jimmy. He didn't notice when a man with a ball cap and bushy beard sat down beside them.

"Hot, isn't it?" the man said to no one in particular.

"Not as hot as it will get," said Hannah. "I hear they don't turn on the misters until it gets to 90."

Max glanced up from his phone. Hannah could always be relied on to do the talking. Max paused when the man lifted his cap to wipe his forehead. Max noticed the underside of the bill was rimmed with small lights. *Weirdness*, Max thought and returned to his texting.

"They didn't have misters when I first started coming here," said the man. "Many things have changed. Most of them for the worse. The park isn't what it used to be."

"Why would you say that?" said Hannah. "Scientopia is one of the most popular theme parks in the country."

"Theme park," said the man. "That's it, isn't it? This wasn't supposed to be a theme park. It's an ongoing science exhibition. More like a permanent world's fair. Hunter doesn't know what he's doing. All show and no science since Hoff left. It has become just like any other entertainment. He'll wreck the place before it's over."

"You mean Steve?" asked Hannah.

The man snorted. "What do you think young man?"

Max looked up from his phone. "I think it's great," he said.

"You here for the day?"

"We're participating in the Summer Genius program. We'll be here all summer," said Hannah.

The man seemed annoyed that Hannah had answered. He looked directly at Max. "That sounds important. Your mother must be proud of you."

Max barely looked up from his phone and without thinking said, "I don't have a mom, just a dad."

"I'm sorry to hear that...what's your name?"

"Max," he said with his eyes still glued to his phone.

"I used to know a woman with a boy called Max. Her name was Katherine Powers. She worked here in the park with me."

Max's looked up, his eyes wide. "That was my mom!"

The man looked surprised. He gazed more intently at Max. "You know, now that you mention it, I can see the resemblance. Your eyes are different, but the mannerisms are the same. How's your dad doing? I knew him, too."

"He's fine," said Max, burning to know more.

The man continued. "You know, Max, it occurs to me that we may be able to help each other. I bet you know a lot about the park, don't you?"

Max nodded. He was beginning to feel uncomfortable.

"I could help you and your father. All I want is information. Things you know. There's a lot of money involved. You could be rich."

Max stood up and said, "I don't think so." He saw that Hannah was nervous and confused as she stood up.

"Wait! Please hear me out," said the man.

As Max turned to leave, the man grabbed his wrist.

"Let me go." Max said quietly.

"Not on your life kid. We have work to do."

Max tried to pull away, but the man was too strong.

The man pulled Max toward some nearby bushes. Max knew the bushes concealed an entrance to the service tunnels. If he was trapped down there, there's no telling what could happen. Max pulled harder and yelled, "Help!"

Where was Hannah? He turned just in time to see her deliver a kick to the man's right shin. The man groaned and turned to face Hannah. Max broke free of the man's grip, lost his balance and fell to the ground. The man lunged at him.

"Come on!" yelled Hannah as she moved around behind the attacker and grabbed Max's hand. She pulled him up, and they ran. It took Max a couple of seconds to fully regain his balance and then he took the lead, dragging Hannah along. He could sense the man pursuing, just a few steps behind them.

Max scanned frantically for somewhere to go. He saw a crowd leaving the Constellation Theater and charged straight into the throng. Max glanced back and saw that the man was having a hard time making his way through the crowd, but he was still too close.

Max and Hannah plunged forward through the open auditorium doors. The theater was empty as they sprinted down the aisle toward the stage. Before they had covered a dozen meters, Max looked over his shoulder and saw their pursuer explode into the room.

"This way!" panted Max. He led Hannah to the steps leading up to the stage. As they leaped onto the platform, Max surveyed their surroundings. There were two ways out. Double doors on each side of the stage, one set a few steps away and another set on the far wall. The bearded man was approaching fast. In a few seconds, he would reach them. Max pulled Hannah toward the closest exit.

They hit at full speed. The doors flew open and banged against the walls on either side. They turned right and raced down a bare cinderblock corridor, lit by fluorescent lights. As Max and Hannah reached the end of the corridor they heard the sound of the bearded man colliding with the doors they had just come through.

The corridor ended in a T-intersection. Max quickly looked both ways, turned right, and ran with Hannah close behind him. He stopped abruptly at the first door on the left. Hannah grabbed the doorknob, but it would not turn.

"It's locked!" said Hannah, with panic in her voice.

43

Max flattened his palm against the security pad mounted on the wall next to the door. There was a split-second delay and a synthetic voice said, "Hello, Mr. Hoff."

They heard a metallic *click* and Max pushed the door open, dragging Hannah inside.

CHAPTER 6

Max and Hannah were greeted by a scream of surprise. They had entered a medium-sized room with an overstuffed couch and matching chairs against one wall and a large vanity with a huge lighted mirror against the other. There were several free-standing racks of girl's clothes. Standing between them and the closest rack was a beautiful girl in her underwear. She was the one screaming. "What are you doing here? Get out!" she shrieked as she reached for a towel to cover herself.

Max recognized her immediately. It was Kaylee. His face flushed red.

"A man was chasing us. We were trying to get away," Max said.

Kaylee picked up a tablet that had been lying on the vanity. She tapped the screen twice and said, "There's nobody there." She turned the tablet around so Max and Hannah could see a security camera feed from the corridor they had just run through. "I'm tired of people trying to bust into my dressing room. I'm calling security."

"No, really," said Hannah. "We're with the Summer Genius program. We had milkshakes at the Galaxy Grill and then a man tried to pull us into the bushes. He chased us into the theater, and we ended up here."

Kaylee seemed to relax a little. "So, you're the smart kids? I'm doing a show for you tomorrow."

"I've been watching your YouTube videos since before you were famous," Max blurted as he turned an even brighter shade of red. "I thought you should have won Talent America. You were so much better than Carmen."

Kaylee smiled. "Thank you, you're sweet."

"How did you get in here?" asked Kaylee. "That door is only supposed to let my mother and me in."

"Max has special powers," said Hannah.

"What?" asked Kaylee. "Like Spiderman or something?"

"No, he just knows everything about the park. And it knows him!"

There was a buzzing at the door. Kaylee looked at the screen. It was Alistair. "See?" said Kaylee, "Even Alistair can't get in, I wonder what he wants?"

Kaylee opened the door.

"I'm sorry to disturb you, Kaylee," said Alistair. "I've been sent to retrieve Max and Hannah. I hope this hasn't been an inconvenience."

Kaylee shrugged.

"Bye," said Max and Hannah in unison as they were leaving. "Sorry," Max added as the door closed.

"What was that all about?" said Hannah as they followed Alistair out of the Constellation Theater. "Since when do you know anything about pop stars? You could barely speak. You like her don't you? Did you see how long and straight her hair is?" she said without pausing.

Hannah pulled her curls from the side of her face and looked at them. "It's not fair. I'm the only Asian I know with curly hair. You don't really like her, do you? She's silly, don't you think?"

Max didn't respond. He was still thinking of Kaylee behind that towel.

"Where are we going?" Hannah asked Alistair.

"I am taking you to Steve."

At hearing Steve's name, Max snapped back to reality. He had the sinking feeling that Steve wouldn't be happy about them storming into Kaylee's dressing room.

"Are we in trouble?" asked Hannah. She could be counted on to ask the questions.

"I don't know what Steve wants," said Alistair.

They went into the nearest APT station and got in line. When they got to the head of the line, they stepped onto a moving conveyor belt that matched the speed of the still moving APT car and climbed aboard. "Crystal Tower," Alistair said as they took their seats. At each end of the car, there was a medium-sized touchscreen that displayed their route and destination. You could make changes by tapping the screens or by speaking.

As their car cleared the station, it merged with the flow of APT traffic and moved along the elevated roadway toward the Crystal Tower. APTs could travel on the streets below, but at a much slower speed.

A few minutes later they arrived at the Crystal Tower station. It was a short walk from the APT station to the Crystal Tower elevator. Steve's office was located at the pinnacle of the Crystal Tower. Access to Steve's office was restricted to certain people and ani-droids, including Alistair. The elevator read Alistair's embedded RFID chip and took them directly to their destination without stopping on any other floors.

Steve Hunter's office occupied the entire top floor of the Crystal Tower. It was encased within a transparent dome that provided a fantastic panoramic view of Scientopia and the surrounding countryside. A narrow catwalk was visible outside the dome.

Max and Hannah had barely settled into their seats in the reception area when Steve came in to welcome them. Steve extended his hand to Hannah and said, "Ah, you would be…"

"Hannah."

Max noticed that without his glasses, Steve's powers were much diminished.

"Yes, of course. It's a pleasure to see you. Would you like to see the view from the catwalk? It's quite breathtaking."

Hannah nodded.

"Awesome, Alistair will escort you." Steve turned to Max.

"I'm very glad to see you, Max. Join me in my office."

Max walked into Steve's inner office and was surprised at what he saw. Instead of a boring grown up office, it looked like a high-tech man cave. Old school video games lined one wall and a three-hole putting green ran along the floor to ceiling windows that overlooked the gigantic Crystal Tower atrium. Large blank screens covered almost every square inch of the walls. As Max stepped closer, they lit up with a variety of bizarre, abstract art. Max cocked his head and tried to make sense of the pictures.

"Interesting," said Steve as he smiled. "Kandinsky and Kurt Schwitters. You have very sophisticated tastes."

"But I didn't pick these," Max said. "They just came on by themselves."

"The art in this office is interactive. The program picks artwork based on what a guest's particular interest might be. We use their Internet searches and any relevant information from social media." Steve studied Max for a moment. "Most children who visit my office have pictures of cartoon or video game characters." Steve looked closely at the artwork. "The last time I saw this painting was..." Steve stopped mid-sentence as the smile faded from his face.

Steve took a deep breath, turning back to Max, and asked him to have a seat.

"I hope you're settling in here at Scientopia. Are you recovered from the incident yesterday?"

Max nodded.

"That was unfortunate. We've never had anything like that happen with a helmet before. Do you have any idea what may have caused it?"

"Not really," said Max, almost in a whisper.

"What about the incident this afternoon with the bearded man, do you know anything about him?" asked Steve.

Max shook his head. He wondered how much Steve knew about what had happened.

"Did the man say what he wanted from you?"

"He said he would give me money for information."

"What kind of information?"

"He didn't say."

Steve looked at Max carefully as if he was trying to decide what to make of him. "Do you know who that man is?"

Max looked up. Now he was curious. "No," he said.

"If I told you his name is Sergey Mamontov, would that mean anything to you?"

Again, Max shook his head.

Steve paused as if considering how to proceed. "Mamontov, along with Verner Hoff and myself, founded Hoff Enterprises. He was a silent partner. Verner was the business and science part of the team. I was the visionary, and Sergey focused on the systems and technology. He was a reclusive sort of man who didn't like public attention. Over time, his eccentricities became difficult to deal with, and we used a clause in the operating agreement to ease him out of management. He felt he had been unjustly removed and is dedicated to causing trouble for Hoff Labs and Scientopia. He's a dangerous man, Max, and if you see him again you should contact me immediately. Can you do that for me?"

Max nodded.

Steve smiled. "A man of few words I see. I like that."

"Could I get you something to drink? How about a smoothie?"

Max didn't know what a smoothie was, but it sounded a lot like a milkshake and he was done with those for the day. "A soda would be good."

Steve pressed a button in the arm of his chair and asked for his robot assistant to bring in a soda. "You really should reconsider drinking those things," he said to

Max. "Do you have any idea what they do to your teeth and the rest of your body? I recommend flavored waters. In fact, I'll have one right now. I'll get one for you to try as well." Steve pressed the button in his armrest again. "Shelia, will you bring in two maple waters as well?"

"Why do you think, Max, that a technical genius like Sergey Mamontov would want information from a boy such as yourself? Don't you think that odd?"

"I guess," said Max.

"Do you have any idea what he might want?"

"Not really," said Max. Max did have an idea, and despite trying his best to look uninformed, he was sure Steve saw the guilt in his eyes.

Steve nodded. "Max, what do you know about Project Gemini?"

Max felt like he was being cornered.

"Not much," Max was telling the truth.

"But when you had the helmet on you said 'Project Gemini.' What made you say that?"

"I have no idea. It just came to me."

"Did other things come to you as well?"

"Yes."

"Things that you don't understand and didn't know before?"

"Yes."

"I see. Come with me, Max."

They walked to some stairs and climbed to a tree-house-like platform in the center of the office. It allowed for an even greater view outside the dome. Max saw Alistair and Hannah out on the catwalk. Max felt a little bit like the floor was falling, but he realized that it was just his fear of heights. He closed his eyes and took a deep breath, trying to steady himself. After a few moments, he was able to relax and focus on the magnificent view.

Steve and Max stood for a while, gazing at the park below. Most of the park was visible from this vantage point. Max could see from the front gates to the twin rockets that dominated Spaceland at the very back of the park. Max realized that he hadn't made it to that part of the park yet.

"Scientopia is an impressive place isn't it, Max?"

"It's wonderful," said Max.

"I'm glad you think so. But not everything is as it seems. It requires an enormous amount of money to run a place like Scientopia. Many people depend on the park for their jobs, and we have to attract an ever-increasing number of guests to pay the bills. Do you understand that?"

"Yes. It looks like there are a lot of people here."

"There are, but appearances can be deceiving. There's a lot of competition for people's entertainment dollars these days: tablets, smartphones, video games, movies. To attract customers, we have to offer things they can't find anywhere else. Science just isn't the draw that it used to be."

"It's exciting to me."

"I know it is Max, and that's one of the reasons we bring in people like you and your fellow scholars, to help us find the excitement. But it's not enough. Have you seen every exhibit and show yet, or just ridden all the rides?"

Max looked down in embarrassment. "Almost all." He looked out at Spaceland sheepishly.

"Yes, Spaceland is one of the least-visited sections of the park now. Most people aren't interested in space anymore. I'd tear it down, but Mr. Hoff is buried there."

Max had heard rumors that Mr. Hoff had himself frozen after he died, but finding out that he was buried in the park was a little creepy.

"There used to be three rockets, but we removed one in Mr. Hoff's honor," Steve continued. "I wasn't very keen on it, but it was his wish. And now, it's just a reminder of what used to be cool."

Max was feeling uncomfortable. He knew Steve wanted something from him, but he didn't know what it was. "What can I do?" Max asked.

"I wish more of the people I meet with would ask that question, Max. I can tell already that you have gifts that would fit in well in a place like Scientopia." Steve took a deep breath.

"Max, you seem to know things about the park that others don't. We don't know why that is, but we would like for you to work with us to see if we can uncover information that may be useful to Scientopia. Does that sound good?"

Max wanted to shout "Yes!" but something made him hesitate.

"Maybe," said Max. "But what is Project Gemini?"

Steve smiled, "Good question, Max. I wish I knew. It was something Mr. Hoff and Sergey were working on before Sergey left and Mr. Hoff died. We believe it was a technology to help take the park to the next level, and it probably has other applications as well. Sergey is now our enemy and Mr. Hoff is gone, but it seems like you may be able to help us find some of the answers. Will you help?"

Max wanted to help more than anything. He had a feeling that answering Steve's questions would answer his as well. Perhaps he could even find out more about what had happened to his mother. Max didn't know why, but all of this was related.

"Yes," said Max.

Steve smiled broadly. "Good. I knew we could count on you."

CHAPTER 7

It was obvious that Max knew more about Javascript than today's instructor. Instead of wasting his time pretending to pay attention he was focused on something else.

Kaylee was putting on a special show later for the Summer Geniuses followed by a private reception. It was almost the only thing Max had been able to think about since he got up. He felt his face get warm at the memory of her standing there in that towel. Max hoped his face hadn't turned red.

Max felt a sting on the back of his neck. He turned his head and came eye to eye with Ryan and his superior attitude. Ryan was shooting spitballs again. Max didn't know whether to feel anger or pity. Why was he always the target? He knew Ryan was being childish, and that the best thing would be to ignore him. On the other hand, he felt humiliated and wondered if letting Ryan have his way made everyone else see him as a victim.

More importantly, did tolerating Ryan make him *feel* like a victim?

Max remembered the stupid anti-bullying program at school. He had been told that bullies acted out because of their own problems. If that was true, what good did knowing it do? It wasn't like he was going to try and start a friendship with Ryan to help him with his problems. He couldn't imagine what kinds of problems someone as rich, confident, and good-looking as Ryan might have. Max decided for the ten-thousandth time that grown-ups didn't have a clue about being a kid. He wondered if a mind wipe came with a driver's license, keeping adults from remembering what it was like being a kid.

Max's mind drifted to the other big thing for the day: starting the Project Gemini work with Steve. This was an exciting prospect. It was difficult to imagine working alongside one of the world's most famous visionaries. It didn't seem real.

Neither did Project Gemini.

After sorting through the memories and images he received while wearing the virtual reality helmet, Max still didn't have any idea of what Gemini was. The only thing he could dig up was what looked like a library citation, and that didn't make sense at all. Max had a feeling he was going to let Steve, and everyone else, down.

Max realized Hannah was jabbing him in the arm. "Max, he's calling on you," she said.

"What?" replied Max.

"Max," said Dr. Venable, "are you paying attention? You're going to need this information to complete your project. I asked what are the possible attributes for variable scope?"

"Global and local," said Max.

Dr. Venable looked a bit surprised; "Yes, that's correct. Good, Max."

Hannah gave Max a questioning look. Dr. Venable went back to talking about something or another, and Max fell once again into the mysteries of Project Gemini.

Dr. Greg Symonds bent down and adjusted the helmet on Max's head. "How's that Max?" he asked.

"It feels OK," said Max as he looked at Steve. "What is it I'm looking for again?"

Steve bent down to be at eye-level with Max and said, "Anything about Project Gemini. Documents, hardware, something that will let us know more about what it is."

Max nodded. "OK," he said.

Max was more than a little nervous about wearing the helmet. "What if it starts to hurt?" he asked.

Greg pointed once again to the screen in front of them. "We're monitoring the data throughput right here. If it gets too high or looks like it's going to spike, I'll sever the connection, and we'll remove the helmet. Just tell me what you're feeling. We can stop anytime you like. Sound good?"

Max nodded again. He was glad Greg was there. "I'm ready," he said.

As he pulled his visor down, Max thought both Steve and Greg looked nervous.

The world inside Max's head lit up: random images and sounds. He closed his eyes, tried to relax, and cautiously opened them again. Slowly the images became clearer. Max looked around.

"What do you see?" asked Steve.

"Wait," said Max. Max didn't recognize the room. As he scanned his surroundings, he saw walls lined with bookshelves. "I think I'm in a library," said Max.

"Describe it," said Steve.

Max moved toward one of the shelves. He chose a book at random and read the title printed on the spine. It was labeled *Crystal Tower Electrical Systems Manual*. He pulled it off the shelf and opened it up. A sharp, brief pain went through his head. Max winced.

"Whoa. You okay?" asked Greg.

Max didn't know if he was okay, but he nodded anyway.

"What were you doing Max?" asked Steve.

"Opening a book," replied Max.

"Did it hurt?" asked Greg.

"A little," said Max.

"You must have downloaded the whole thing at once," said Greg. "Try opening another one. This time, see if you can limit the download to one page at a time. Try to control the data transfer rate."

Max replaced the electrical manual and pulled down a different volume, *Costume Sketches for Thanksgiving Parade*. As Max slowly opened the book, he felt a *push* inside his head. He concentrated and pushed back. This time there was no pain.

"Good, Max," said Greg. "It started to spike but you stopped it. Whatever you did, keep doing it."

"Can you still see what's in the books?" asked Steve.

"Yes."

"What do you see now?"

Max flipped his way through the costume book and described its contents.

"What other titles do you see?"

Max started announcing titles out loud: Operating Procedures for APTs, Local Marketing Plan, Safety Training Syllabus, and his favorite, Secret Dessert Recipes.

"It sounds like he's in the corporate document repository," said Steve. "Max, do you see anything that looks like Project Gemini?"

"No. There doesn't seem to be any order to the books."

"Is there any way to search?" asked Greg. "Something like a card catalog?"

"I don't know what that is," said Max. "I don't see anything, but I think I can search through the titles."

Max closed his eyes and focused on the phrase **Project Gemini**. When he opened his eyes again, a new volume had appeared on the shelf in front of him. He read the title: *Project Gemini Overview*.

Max opened the book and felt a sharp pain. "Ow," he said. He had forgotten to control the download and had been overwhelmed by the contents of the book rushing into his head all at once. He realized that with the book in his head he could search all of the contents at once rather than flipping through page by page.

"I think I found something," said Max. "It looks like a description of Project Gemini."

"Tell me what it says," said Steve.

Max read through the title page, a blurb about mission and values that didn't mean anything to him and an objective that was equally as vague. Then, when he got to the section titled *Project Contacts* his heart jumped. There, on a line with the title Program Manager, was the name Katherine Powers, his mother.

"What is it Max?" asked Greg.

For whatever reason, he didn't want to reveal his find to Steve. "Nothing," Max said. "I lost my place." Max continued reading the Table of Contents and the rest of the information in the book. Most of it was boring and non-helpful stuff such as reporting procedures and resource prioritization. When Max got to the section titled *Deliverables*, it got interesting.

The first several deliverables were yawners—more reports. Max was quickly coming to the conclusion that, even in a theme park, the first priority was paperwork and reports. But there it was, under subsection E, the description: "One prototype ani-droid based on optical chips with embedded artificial intelligence, powered by hydrogen fuel cells driving electromechanical limbs; to be named Alistair."

"I found it!"

"What Max? What did you find?" asked Steve.

Max ripped off the helmet. "I know what Project Gemini is. It's Alistair!"

CHAPTER 8

When Max returned to his room he immediately logged into Roblox and began searching for a worthy opponent to practice his sword fighting skills. He was starting to get the hang of wearing the VR helmet and navigating through Scientopia's computer systems, but it was exhausting, especially compared to the ease with which he moved around in Roblox.

Roblox was a friend; always waiting for him with fun, adventure, and companionship. No matter what sort of mood he was in, Roblox had something to match it. If he wanted to be alone, he could work on world building. If that seemed too tedious, he could work on recruiting more players into his group. If he wanted to be around people, he could play games and chat. Sometimes he just wanted to cut loose and chop up other players.

Tonight, Max was looking for players he could slice and dice with his virtual blade. Others might prefer guns but not Max. His sword required much more skill. The primary challenge was finding someone good enough to put up a decent fight. It was fun slaying everyone in sight for about the first fifteen minutes; then you wanted someone who could test your skill. As Max improved, it was getting harder and harder to find players who could challenge him.

After wiping out everyone on his server, Max was getting bored. That's when he noticed NetTechGuy486 at the far end of the base, whacking all comers. *"One more,"* said Max to himself.

Max hopped over to NetTechGuy486 and launched a direct attack. Instantly, NetTechGuy486 dodged and counter-attacked, leaving Max in pieces. NetTechGuy486 texted, "You noob." Max laughed. It had been a long time since anyone had called him a noob. This one was *good*.

As Max waited to regenerate, he considered what his next strategy should be. His direct attack had failed, something more advanced was necessary. He decided on a jumping attack: running directly at his opponent and leaping over him and striking from the rear. It was an easy attack to counter if you knew what you were doing. This was a good way to see if NetTechGuy486 had just gotten lucky.

As soon as he regenerated, Max made his move. He charged directly at NetTechGuy486. Just before he was in range of his opponent's weapon Max jumped.

Instead of sailing gracefully over NetTechGuy486's head, Max, once again found himself in pieces. Dead. "*Loser,*" NetTechGuy486 taunted him. "*If u can't do better, I'm leaving.*"

Max twitched in irritation. He was going to have to step up his game.

After regenerating Max charged again. He had briefly considered waiting for NetTechGuy486 to attack, but decided that offense was best.

This time, at the last possible instant, he stepped aside, turned, and brought his blade down hard. It looked good, but unbelievably NetTechGuy486 blocked him and struck back. Max parried and pushed forward trying to keepNetTechGuy486 off balance. This attack was successful but just barely. He managed to inflict a wound.

They continued circling each other, searching for weakness, trading blows, neither able to inflict a killing stroke. Their lives were quickly draining away. Max was weakening faster than his opponent. He was running out of time. In desperation, Max managed to land a blow that knocked NetTechGuy486 to the ground.

"*LOL!*" Max texted.

"The force is strong with U," NetTechGuy486 texted.

"*U2,*" Max replied.

"Let's start over, Max."

Max's smile faded. How did NetTechGuy486 know his real name? Maybe it was one of his friends with a new account.

"*Who dis?*" texted Max.

"*Your mom's friend,*" came the reply.

Max froze. It was Sergey. He stared at the keyboard and blinking cursor, wondering what to do. He wanted to yell for help, but that seemed silly. They were online. You couldn't get hurt on Roblox; it was just a game.

Max thought about logging off, but he wanted to know more about his mom, and Sergey said he had answers.

CHAPTER 9

Max was trying to work up some enthusiasm about Kaylee's show. But as the rest of the crowd filed into the Constellation Theater his online conversation with Sergey weighed on his mind. If Sergey had been telling the truth, there was much more to Project Gemini than he had imagined. Max desperately wanted to talk to someone about what he had been told.

"Why do we have to be here?" Hannah asked. "No one who appreciates music listens to Kaylee."

Max looked at Hannah as if she were an alien. Sometimes she seemed so strange. Always talking, always giving opinions.

Hannah took his look as a question. "I should know," she said. "I've been playing the violin since I was five. You can't put pop music in the same category, and Kaylee's songs hardly qualify as pop music. It's not much more than noise."

Hannah was a superb talker. Max wondered if she could be an equally skilled listener.

"I talked with Sergey last night," Max said to Hannah quietly.

"You what? Where? You're not supposed to do that; he's dangerous."

"Not in person, online. He was on Roblox."

"How did he find you on Roblox? He knows too much, Max. You should stay away from him. Tell Steve."

Max sighed and settled deeper into his seat. "I don't know; Sergey says not to tell anyone."

"Of course, he does," said Hannah, her eyes growing big. "That's what all cyber stalkers say. You need to tell Steve."

"He says he knows something about my mom. If I tell I won't find out."

Hannah looked at Max disapprovingly. Max had expected that reaction. She was probably right, but it wasn't what he wanted to hear. Max pushed his head against the back of his seat and looked up at the ceiling of the theater. It was comforting to see star patterns like those that adorned his bedroom ceiling.

"What's up, Max?" asked Hannah.

"Look, there's an extra star."

"Where?" asked Hannah. Astronomy was Hannah's strong suit, so she was surprised that Max would notice something about the stars that she hadn't seen.

"Right there," said Max, pointing.

Before Hannah could find it, the lights dimmed, and music filled the theater. *Kaylee Live* had started.

Despite Hannah's lack of enthusiasm, Max thought Kaylee's performance was impressive. It seemed to Max that she was almost sparkling. He could feel her energy. Seeing her live was so much better than YouTube. When Max watched her videos online, she was performing on small stages and at county fairs. Scientopia's Constellation Theater was a different world. Every song was perfectly synched with holograms and lasers. About half way through the show camera drones buzzed the audience, transmitting close-ups of the fans onto the large screen behind Kaylee and her dancers. As he watched, Max planned what he was going to say to Kaylee at the backstage reception.

As the final song concluded Max was the first one out of his seat, cheering and clapping. He glanced back at Hannah, who was still seated, practically sulking.

"Wasn't that great?" Max shouted over the crowd.

Hannah stood up and clapped halfheartedly. "Yeah, the special effects were okay," she said.

The applause subsided, the lights came up, and people filed out of the theater.

Max waited impatiently for his classmates to clear out of his row. He couldn't comprehend why they were taking so long instead of rushing to the reception. Maybe they didn't understand that it's not every day you get to meet Kaylee. He wondered if he would get a hug when they met.

As he climbed the stairs to the stage, Max could see that a group had already formed around her. He walked past the punch bowl that had been set up just off stage and navigated around two clusters of kids talking loudly. He noticed, with a twinge of irritation, Hannah following him. What was she doing? She thought Kaylee's music was nothing but noise.

Max approached the group surrounding Kaylee. It was mostly girls. Max was hesitant to push his way into a group of girls but decided it was worth it. He got a couple of dirty looks as he moved forward, saying "Excuse me."

When he reached the inner ring, he saw that Kaylee was signing an autograph for Amber Austin. Kaylee was gorgeous in her sequined jumpsuit and makeup. Max couldn't restrain himself.

"Hi, Kaylee, that was a great show!" Even as he said it, he realized she must have heard that ten thousand times already.

A hint of recognition crossed Kaylee's face as she finished Amber's autograph and looked at Max. At that moment, Hannah popped up right beside him.

"Oh, hi…you two. Broken into any dressing rooms lately?"

Max couldn't tell if she was serious or not. It was clear that Kaylee had forgotten his name.

Max felt the crowd loosen up a bit. He didn't want to take his eyes off of Kaylee to find out why. His mind was completely blank as he searched for something else to say.

"Do you always stumble after *Stop Me Now*?" a familiar male voice to Max's left asked, "or was that just for us?"

Kaylee's gaze shifted from Max toward the source of the question. Kaylee blushed. Max turned to see who had ruined his moment with Kaylee, but he knew who it was: Ryan Fairchild.

"I didn't stumble," Kaylee protested with a broad smile.

"So, you're saying you go flying around like that on purpose?" asked Ryan.

"You weren't supposed to notice," she said.

Max felt the moment slipping away. He needed to say something. "It looked perfect to me," he said.

From the look Kaylee and Ryan gave him you would have thought he had spoken in Mandarin Chinese.

"Stick with me, and I'll see that you don't embarrass yourself anymore," said Ryan smugly.

Was Ryan hitting on *Kaylee*? Surely, even he would fail.

"And who are you?" said Kaylee with a sparkle in her eye.

Ryan smirked, raised his eyebrows, and opened his arms to his side as if to say, *isn't it obvious?*

Kaylee laughed.

Max had been hoping for a different reaction. He didn't know what to expect or what was going on. He was feeling more and more like an ant at a picnic.

"Tell you what," Ryan said. "Come with me to the Founder's Ball, and you can see for yourself."

Kaylee smiled and looked back at her personal assistant, who checked her phone and nodded. "Okay," said Kaylee. "Give your number to Beth. It's a date."

Max was crushed. *He* was the fan. He had watched her videos before they'd become popular. He had talked to her first. It should have been him taking her to the

Founder's Ball, not Ryan. Max tried to slink away unseen, but he couldn't get away before Ryan flashed him a condescending smile. He pushed his way out of the circle and ran out of the theater with Hannah close behind.

"Max! What's wrong?" she asked. "Are you mad at Ryan? You don't want to go to the ball with Kaylee, do you? It would be like going with a python. She would get all of the attention, and you would look silly. We can go to the ball together."

Whatever feelings he had about going to the ball with Kaylee, Max didn't want to discuss it with Hannah. She was biased.

"No," Max said, "I just can't stand how Ryan is always trying to one-up me."

Max got a tingling sensation at the base of his skull and grabbed Hannah by the arm to pull her aside as a family of four, all looking at their phones, walked through the space they had been occupying seconds before. These sensations he couldn't explain were starting to annoy him.

Hannah looked at Max with a confused expression. "How did you...?"

Max shrugged in exasperation. "I'm going to talk to Sergey. He seems to be the only one around here who knows what's going on."

"Max, you can't. Steve won't like it."

Max looked at Hannah with determination.

"Okay," said Hannah, "But I'm coming with you."

Sergey responded immediately to Max's IM.

"He wants to meet tonight," Max said to Hannah. "Where do you think we should do it?"

"It needs to be in a public place," said Hannah. "You remember what happened last time. It should be before curfew too. You don't want to get caught out of the dorms; they would probably kick you out of the program."

Max nodded and sent a text telling Sergey to meet him at 7:30 p.m. at the Galaxy Grill.

"I'm going too," said Hannah.

"No, you're not," Max replied.

This time, it was Hannah who gave the determined look.

"Fine. You can come. But you have to sit at another table with a phone. That way if he tries to take me you can call for help."

Max and Hannah got to the grill at 7:15 to check the place out. There was nothing obviously out of place. Max sat at a table in the center of the restaurant. Hannah sat at a table against the wall where she had a clear view of Max.

At 7:35 an old lady approached and sat down at his table. "Um, I'm sorry ma'am, that seat's taken."

The lady didn't move. "Max, it's me, Sergey."

Max leaned closer to get a better look. It sure seemed like an old woman to him. "Why are you dressed like that?"

Sergey rolled his eyes. "They're doing everything they can to keep me out of the park. I have to come in disguise."

Out of the corner of his eye, Max saw Hannah looking at him. He noticed the confusion on her face. He nodded once and turned back to Sergey.

"How did you get so good at Roblox?" he asked.

"I've spent my whole life in a virtual world; learning, working, playing video games. In many ways, I find it superior to the physical world."

"I know what you mean," said Max. "How did you know I was there?"

"There are no secrets online, Max. If you know where to look, how to look, you can learn anything. You would be surprised at the things I could show you."

Max raised his eyebrows. His curiosity was interrupted with a thought.

"If you can find out anything, then why do you need me?" Max asked.

Sergey managed a weak smile through his rubber mask.

"You're a clever boy, Max. I can see why Steve is interested in you. What have you learned about Project Gemini?"

"I found it," said Max. Looking at Sergey, he was surprised to see no response. This was his big news, his bargaining chip to find out more about his mother. He needed for Sergey to be impressed.

"What did you find?" asked Sergey.

"If I tell you, then you will have no reason to tell me about my mom."

Sergey kept staring at Max coolly. He pushed back a stray lock of gray hair.

"You found the *Project Gemini Overview,* didn't you? The one that mentioned your mother and Alistair."

Max couldn't hide the surprise on his face. His secret was no secret at all. "Steve didn't know," Max said.

"Oh yes, he does. He has known for several years. Why do you think he's lavished so much attention on Alistair? He acted like everything you told him was news, didn't he?"

Max nodded.

"He doesn't trust you, Max. He's not trustworthy himself, so he doesn't trust anyone in return."

Max lowered his eyes.

"Disappointing, isn't it? I know the feeling. The jerk took everything from me. I despise him."

Max was surprised at the outburst. "He said you're dangerous."

"I'm sure he did. Did he also tell you that he stole my work and the company I helped found?"

"No."

"I'm sure he didn't. Steve is a manipulator. He only reveals what benefits him. You know that Max, or you wouldn't be here with me, a supposedly dangerous man. Isn't that right?"

"I just want to know about my mom."

Sergey relaxed. "Of course, you do. What would you like to know?"

"What was she doing here?"

"Your father hasn't told you?"

"No," said Max. "He doesn't talk about her much. It makes him sad. And I don't think he likes Scientopia."

"Your father is right to be suspicious of Hoff Enterprises, Max. Steve has turned it into a twisted monster of what Verner intended."

It looked to Max like Sergey was going to launch into a rant about Steve and Scientopia, but he stopped himself.

"Your mother was a brilliant woman, Max. She showed me many kindnesses."

For the first time, he could see softness in Sergey's eyes. More than anything, he wished he could share those thoughts, to see what his mother was like.

"What was her job?" asked Max.

Sergey focused his attention back on Max.

"Her title was vice president of research and development. But like many titles, that was deceptive. She was Verner's special assistant. He gave her tasks he wouldn't trust to anyone else."

"Like Project Gemini?" asked Max.

Sergey nodded.

"Was my mother in charge of Project Gemini?"

"Yes."

Max digested the information. "If Project Gemini is not Alistair, what is it?"

Sergey looked at Max for a moment as if trying to decide whether to trust him. He took a deep breath and said: "Project Gemini was an optical computer chip I was working on. It was--is--revolutionary. I was able to devise a way to build the chip atom by atom to create billions of parallel pathways. Even the first prototype, dubbed Alpha Geminorum, performed an order of magnitude better than anything else available. It has the potential to be thousands, if not millions of times faster than silicon-based processors. With none of the heat generated by traditional chips."

Sergey grasped Max's arm excitedly.

"Do you know what that means Max? The new places we could put chips? Artificial intelligence? There's no limit to the new applications."

Max glanced at Hannah and saw she was looking alarmed, about to use her phone. Max shook his head and mouthed, *It's Okay.*

"Why can't they just use the chip that's in Alistair?" asked Max.

"Several reasons," sighed Sergey. "First, Steve hates taking Alistair offline for any reason. People complain if he's absent. He'd rather trot that silly robot around and make money than to do any real research."

Max felt annoyed that Sergey referred to Alistair as a silly robot, but he kept silent.

"And even if he tried, he'd never be able to figure out how to duplicate the chip. It's too advanced."

"Could you?"

"Yes. Well, not exactly." Sergey scratched his nose as best he could under the mask. "You see, I mainly created the method to make the chip. A sort of a 3D crystal printer. The processing and built-in code was mostly Verner and your mother's doing."

Max listened intently. He never quite knew what his mother did at Scientopia and every new bit of information helped him understand her more.

"But what I could do," Sergey continued, "is use the chip. Not Alistair's prototype, but the real chip. Beta Geminorum. As powerful as the original chip is, this new chip is thousands of times more powerful. With that much computing power, I could..."

"But, why do you need me?" asked Max.

"Because the chip is gone Max. It was finished! We had just completed testing. I left the lab one afternoon, and it was there. I came to work the next morning, and they wouldn't let me in. They escorted me to a conference room in the security office, and a bunch of lawyers told me my services were no longer required. That I was not a part of the company I had helped create!"

"Why?"

"Later that day I found out that Verner had died overnight. I'm sure his death, the missing chip, and my dismissal were all related, but I don't know how."

"Where do you think the chip is?" asked Max.

"That's the odd thing. A couple of months later a squad of police in riot gear knocked down the door of my house. They had a warrant for a computer chip. They tore the place apart looking for it, but I didn't have it. They did it two more times later. Whatever happened to the chip, Hoff Enterprises doesn't know where it is, and someone wants it."

Max was still confused about why Sergey thought he had anything to do with the missing chip. "Do you think my mom took it?" Max asked.

Sergey pursed his lips. "No, Max. I did at first. I went to her house and asked. She wouldn't speak to me. She seemed to be afraid. It was about the same time that your parents got you and I assumed there was some threat to your safety."

Max raised his eyebrows but said nothing. *"...about the same time that your parents got you."* That sounded odd.

"Then what do you want from me?" Max asked.

"So much like your mother," said Sergey. "Always pushing for answers."

Again, Sergey lapsed into thought but quickly pulled himself back.

"I don't know how to say this Max. As a scientist, I know that everything has an explanation, even things that seem impossible. Somehow, you have access to the company computers and systems you shouldn't have. It's almost like magic."

"You have full access, don't you?" asked Max.

"Yes, but not like yours."

"How did you get the access? Didn't they cut you off?"

"Yes, but I designed the system, Max. I worked my way back in. No one knew more about it, except maybe Verner. The people in there now are fools."

Max looked at Sergey in his old lady dress. It seemed another sign of a man who couldn't stay focused and was, perhaps, not to be trusted.

"So, you want the chip?" asked Max.

"Yes."

"And how am I supposed to find it?"

Sergey leaned back in his chair. To Max, he looked agitated. "I don't know," he admitted. "There has to be a way, a reference to it or a clue in some document. Something you have access to."

"I think my access only works when I have the helmet on."

"Then you'll have to get the helmet and bring it to me," said Sergey.

"I can't. They track us. We can't leave the park."

"Then I'll have to come to you."

"I don't know. We'll get caught," said Max.

"Trust me, Max, we can do this."

Max looked more closely at Sergey. A man dressed as a woman. A man he had been warned to avoid. Sergey didn't seem trustworthy. Max thought, *Why should I trust you? What can you tell me that I don't already know? Or that I couldn't find out for myself?*

"What do you know about your mother's death Max?"

"Just that she died in a plane crash." Just thinking about her made him sad. It was almost enough to bring tears.

Sergey reached into his impractically large old lady pocket book and pulled out a manila envelope.

"There's much more Max; it's all in here. Find the chip for me, and you get the envelope."

Sergey paused a moment to let it sink in. "I see what you're doing. I promise you won't find this information in the helmet. It's all offline. The papers in here are probably the only copy. Do we have a deal?"

"I'll see what I can do," said Max.

Max looked at Hannah. When he looked back, Sergey was gone.

Hannah came over to his table. "What are you doing Max?" she asked. "Was that Sergey dressed as an old woman? You're not going to help him, are you?"

"I don't know," said Max.

Sergey was a dangerous, unpredictable man. But Sergey was also the only one who knew what happened to his mother.

CHAPTER 10

"Dad, can you hear me?" asked Max.

There was no response. Max adjusted his Skype settings and tried again.

"How about now?"

"I hear you. How are you doing, son? Are you having fun?" asked Mr. Powers.

"It's Okay," said Max.

"That doesn't sound encouraging. Do you want to come home? You know I'll come get you anytime you want."

"No, it's not that. Just so many things going on. I'm kind of tired."

"I see," said Mr. Powers.

"Dad." Max paused, "What do you know about mom? I mean when she died."

Max could see his dad hesitate and take a deep breath.

"Same as we've always known. She was on that plane that went down in the Gulf of Mexico. Why do you ask?"

"I don't know. I was just thinking. Do you know anything about a man called Sergey Mamontov?"

"Not really. He was an engineer of sorts. He worked at Scientopia with your mother. I met him a time or two."

"Did he seem okay to you?"

"I don't know, I guess. He did come to the house once not long after you were born, and it seemed to upset your mother. What's going on Max?"

"I met him, Dad. He says he knows more about what happened to Mom."

"I see," said Mr. Powers.

Max scratched his head as if trying to get at the questions in there. "He said he'd tell me more if I helped him find some information."

"Are you sure this is a good idea, Max? Sergey sounds odd. Maybe it's best to avoid him."

Max looked down and spoke quietly. "He said something I didn't understand."

"What was that?"

"He said when you and mom 'got me,' not 'when you were born.'"

It was clear that his dad was trying to hide a look of surprise. Mr. Powers didn't respond immediately.

"What did he mean?"

"Do we have to do this now Max? Can't we wait until you get back?"

"No, Dad, I need to know now."

Mr. Powers rested his forehead face down in his palms. "I'm sorry, Max. It was never supposed to happen like this. Your mom and I had always intended to tell you. After she died the time never seemed right."

"Right for what?"

Mr. Powers took a deep breath. "To tell you you're adopted."

The knot that had been growing in Max's stomach since talking with Sergey tightened. He expected the news but wasn't prepared for it. It made sense and confirmed something he had wondered about from time to time.

"Are you okay, Max?"

"I'm not sure. I don't know what to think. I feel..." Max leaned forward on his elbows. He had never seen his dad look this upset before. He wanted to be home, to be safe again. Max felt the knot in his stomach dissolve into queasiness. "I feel sick."

"I'm coming to get you, Max. I'm leaving right now."

"No, Dad, don't. I'll be all right. I need to stay here."

In one way, the news of his being adopted made sense, but in many others, it didn't. He felt so connected to his father and even the mother he had barely known. People had always made comments about how he was so much like one parent or the other. It was inconceivable to Max that he was not a part of them. When his attention returned to the computer screen, Max noticed a tear sliding down his father's cheek.

"Don't cry, Dad." Max felt tears welling up in his own eyes. "Please, Dad, it's okay. I understand."

His father sniffed. "I'm sorry Max. I feel like I've let you down."

Max smiled as tears rolled down his cheeks, too. "That's not true. You're my dad." The thought that this knowledge would somehow change things unnerved him. He didn't want anything to change.

"Don't worry, Max. Knowing doesn't change anything. You have been mine from the moment your mother brought you home. Where you came from has never mattered, and it never will."

Max believed his father, the one person who had never let him down. He knew everything would be all right, but he was disappointed that his dad hadn't trusted him enough to tell him earlier.

"I know. I'm sorry, Dad. I'm fine. Just tired, I need to go to bed."

"I love you, Max."

"I love you, too."

Max turned off the computer and stared at it. He could see his reflection in the dark screen. For the first time in his life, he wondered who he was looking at.

CHAPTER 11

Max was on his way to the restroom to brush his teeth when he passed Alistair in the hall.

"Getting ready for bed, Max?"

"Yeah. What are you doing here?"

"Bed check. You geniuses find many ways to test Scientopia's security."

Max made a mental note that Alistair was a part of the security operation as well. "I didn't know that was part of your job. Hey, what do you do all night? You don't sleep do you?"

"Oh heavens no, I have to have my fuel cells recharged with hydrogen, but that only takes a few minutes. I also have a routine that I usually run at night to compress and archive old files and to purge any unnecessary or repetitive data."

"Don't you get tired? Or need rest?" asked Max.

"No, Max, machines wear out when they reach their design limit, but they don't need rest."

"I wish I didn't have to sleep," said Max.

"And I wish I did," said Alistair.

"Why?"

"Because it would make me more human. I would be better able to understand humans."

"What's there to understand?" asked Max.

"Understanding humans is a never-ending task, Max. And infinity is something that programs aren't able to process. It would take an infinite amount of time to compute!" Alistair grinned at Max, putting him at ease. "And you know, every human is unique."

"You're unique, too," said Max.

"Not for long it would seem."

Max didn't think it was possible, but he felt a note of worry in Alistair. "Do you mean our projects?"

Alistair nodded.

"Oh, don't worry about that. Even if we were able to create a perfect replica, it still wouldn't be you." Max put his hand on Alistair's arm to comfort him. It was the first time he had purposely touched Alistair, and he was surprised to feel hard plastic under his clothes instead of soft flesh.

"Thank you, Max, but I am nothing but parts and electrical charges that can easily be replicated."

"But you have experiences that make you unique," said Max.

"And they are all stored as ones and zeros that can be copied to any other electronic device."

"Oh," said Max. He didn't believe it was that simple, but he didn't know how to argue the point. It was something he felt. The feeling made him remember the conversation he had just had with his father.

Alistair pulled his coat flap back. "Would you like a Hoffpop? They come in seven flavors of sweet, fruity, goodness," said Alistair.

Max looked at Alistair's large eyes. He knew they were just glass, but somehow they appeared sympathetic. He needed to tell someone what he had discovered, and at the moment, Alistair seemed a good choice.

"My father just told me I'm adopted." For a moment, he looked into Alistair's eyes, then dropped his gaze to the floor.

"So, you're wondering where you came from?" asked Alistair.

Max looked back up and nodded.

"I understand your feelings. However, does it make a difference? Does this new information change who you are now?"

Max thought about it. Alistair had a point. But it seemed odd to be taking advice from a device. Did it make a difference that the logic was programmed into a machine rather than a person? Isn't a person just a complicated machine?

"No, I suppose you're right." Max brightened.

Alistair brightened too at Max's response. "You get on to bed then; you need your rest for class tomorrow."

Dr. Dieter Lehrer called the morning class to attention. It was unusual for him to start the day, one of the instructors or Alistair usually did that. In fact, Lehrer had been conspicuously absent the last few days.

"Today is a special day," Dr. Lehrer said. "We have finished with our classroom work, and now we will start on the fun part, building our ani-droids. As I have said before, the team that constructs the best ani-droid will win the Hoff Prize. But that raises the question, what would make for the best ani-droid? In other words, what performance standards will you be measured against?"

An excited murmur flashed through the classroom.

"You have heard, I take it, of the Turing test?"

No one raised their hand or showed any hint of recognition. Lehrer waited silently. Finally, Neil Singh blurted out: "A test for artificial intelligence?"

"That's right Mr. Singh. Do you know what the test is?"

"The ability for a machine to fool a human into thinking it's a human?"

"That's correct. I bring it up because everyone wishes to impose the Turing test on us and I do not like it. It is not a test of intelligence, only if a machine can act like a human. Most humans are not intelligent."

There were a few smug laughs in the class.

"And what if a machine was more intelligent than a human? Then to pass the test it would have to play stupid so as not to surpass its human evaluator." Dr. Lehrer looked around the room slowly. "So, I hope that settles any doubts as to why we are not going to be using the Turing test to evaluate your success. Are there any questions?"

No one spoke or raised their hand.

"Good. Then what ani-droid characteristics are important to us? Let's consider Alistair."

Alistair scanned the room with an expression of mock surprise. Several of the children laughed.

"Alistair is an ani-droid with specific tasks to perform. He must be able to greet and interact with our guests. He must understand their questions and provide solutions to their problems. Most difficult of all he must entertain them while performing those tasks, which means he must have a sense of humor."

Dr. Lehrer stopped and smiled as if saying "humor" was funny.

"As you will see, these tasks, while specific, must be employed in a wide range of different contexts with people of widely varied communication abilities. So here are the events and evaluation criteria we will be using to judge your efforts. Alistair, display the contest matrix please."

A slide appeared on the overhead screen. It had three events listed: Knowledge Test, Park Greeter, and Performance.

"Of the three challenges," Dr. Lehrer continued, "the knowledge test is the easiest. All of your ani-droids will be asked the same questions and will receive points for correct answers. The Park Greeter exercise will be far more challenging because it will involve actual service as a greeter at the entrance to the park. The tasks presented will be random and unpredictable because the circumstances will be uncontrolled. The final test will be a live scripted show with Kaylee, where the ani-droids will have to perform as a part of the dance chorus. The team that accumulates the most points will be declared the winner."

Alistair giggled.

"Alistair, would you please be still?" said Hannah as she tried to figure out how to reattach his leg panel.

"I can't help it. I'm not used to being...naked like this."

"Don't be silly; it's just plastic. Like a Barbie doll," said Hannah, still focusing intently on trying to push the panel back into place.

"I don't know if that's a good comparison," said Aiden. "I think Jimmy likes looking at his sister's naked Barbie dolls."

Jimmy blushed. "Do not."

"Aiden, please quit horsing around and help me with this. Does this just snap on or was there a screw in it?" Hannah asked.

"Let me see it," said Jimmy. "It snaps, like this." They heard a *pop* as the panel slid back into place.

"Ah, that feels good," said Alistair.

Jimmy sighed. "Silly robot. That can't feel good; there's no sensor there."

"Whatever it is, my processors are less stressed with all my pieces in place," said Alistair. "I hope the other groups don't wish to take me apart as well."

Max looked up from his computer. "I think the other groups have different ideas." He glanced through the glass partition to Team Turing and locked eyes with Ryan. Max quickly looked away, which gave Ryan even more reason to come over for a visit.

"Having trouble over here?" Ryan said with a smile as he walked in. "I don't know if Alistair is going to survive you people. Look, someone put his stomach panel on upside down."

"Oh my," said Alistair looking at his abdomen.

Hannah blushed and pulled the panel off. "I knew that."

Ryan rolled his eyes. "I don't know why you're messing with this relic anyway. It looks like something from when my dad was a kid. Big head, goofy expressions, ears sticking out." Ryan flicked Alistair's ear as he said that last part, just as Neil was coming in to join the fun.

"Hey," said Hannah. "Don't do that. And don't talk about Alistair like that, he can hear you."

"So?" said Ryan. "It's just a machine. You don't worry about hurting your car's feelings, do you?"

"It's not the same," said Hannah as she pursed her lips and a shot an angry look in Ryan's direction.

"Whatever. It's not going to matter. This thing is a technological dead end. People now want badass. *Halo* and *Call of Duty*, not *The Muppets*. Isn't that right Neil?"

"Yeah, boss."

Max had to admit to himself he was beginning to have doubts about their strategy. It had seemed a good idea, and his teammates had agreed, to use Alistair's mechanics and appearance. That would give them more time to focus on software and performance. But as he looked over to the Team Turing station, and the shiny shell they were putting together, Max felt like his team was a couple of decades behind.

"Yeah, well you still have to make that thing work," said Hannah.

"That's our secret weapon," said Ryan. "I have a feeling that our man is going to put on a rocking performance."

"How are you going to do that?" asked Aiden.

"Connections," said Ryan with a grin. "I happen to know that a certain little hottie will be helping us out personally."

Max was sure Ryan was bringing up Kaylee to rub his nose in it. Max had humiliated Ryan with the sword fight; this was his payback.

"That's not fair!" said Hannah.

"Since when does fair mean anything? Hasn't your daddy told you life's not fair?"

Ryan and Neil laughed as they turned and walked back to their station.

Max, and his fellow Team Ritchie members, were silent while gloom took hold. Max looked at Alistair who was displaying his best sympathetic expression. "Would you like a Hoffpop?" Alistair asked. "It comes in seven flavors of sweet, fruity goodness." He reached to open his coat which usually held the Hoffpops, only to realize that he wasn't wearing anything.

"Oh my," said Alistair looking around for his clothes. "Now this is embarrassing."

Max and his teammates laughed.

CHAPTER 12

Max and Hannah were finishing up dinner in the atrium food court and chatting with Alistair.

"Do you want to ride the Pulsar, Max?" asked Hannah. "I hear it's a lot of fun."

"I can't," said Max. "I have to go work with Steve and the VR helmet."

"What's wrong?" asked Hannah.

"Nothing," said Max with a shrug. "I just haven't been able to find what he's looking for."

"Are you ready to go, Max?" asked Alistair.

"You don't have to come," said Max. "I know the way."

"Yes, but students don't have access to the executive floors, I'll need to sign you in," said Alistair.

"I have access," said Max.

"Yes, well, I'll come anyway," said a flustered Alistair.

Max had become accustomed to the ride up to Steve's office. Since the first session in the lab, Steve had moved the VR helmets to his office for more privacy. Everyone had access to the lab, but Steve's office was secure.

"Here you are Max," said Alistair at the entrance to Steve's office. "I'll be waiting here for you when you're finished."

"Can't you come in?" asked Max.

"I'm not allowed to stay when dropping off a guest for Steve unless Steve invites me," said Alistair.

"Oh," said Max as he walked into the office, looking at the brilliant colors of the sunset. Max imagined it was like being in a cathedral with the stained glass windows aglow.

"Hi Max, are we going to find something tonight?"

Max lowered his head. Steve was so intense. Looking him in the eyes was hard.

"I hope so."

"I do, too. You run on up to the loft and get settled in. Greg is already up there," said Steve.

"Hello Max," said the always-chipper Greg Symonds. "How's your ani-droid project going? Are we going to be impressed at Friday's progress check?"

"I don't know," said Max. It was becoming a sore subject with him. Progress was agonizingly slow, and he was beginning to doubt that anything would be working on the Alistair clone by Friday. "We're having problems."

"With what?"

"Everything."

"Don't worry, Max. It's probably not as bad as it seems. Things tend to come together at the last moment. Don't be afraid to ask if you need help."

Max nodded, and Greg lowered the helmet onto his head.

"Feel okay?" asked Greg.

"Yes." Steve came up the stairs and into the loft. "Are you ready, Max? We need to make some progress tonight. Let's go."

Greg tapped the keys of the computer, and Max found himself in the same library he'd visited in all the previous sessions with Steve.

"Are you in the library?" asked Greg.

"Yes."

"Does anything look different?" asked Steve.

"No."

"What do you see?" asked Steve.

"Just a bunch of books."

"Are any labeled with Project Gemini?"

"No." Max was feeling frustrated. It was the same thing, the same stupid questions every time. He had wandered hundreds of rows, searching every way he knew how, and he had found only one document related to Project Gemini. According to Sergey, Steve already knew about that.

"Max, is there a perimeter you can walk around? See if you can do that," said Greg.

At least this was a new idea. Max was beginning to think Steve and Greg were the problem.

Max moved around the library, from one end to the other, blank gray walls surrounded him. There was no way in or out. He was starting to feel trapped. "I don't see anything," he said.

"Concentrate Max! There has to be something there," said Steve. "Go around again." Max heard the frustration in his voice.

"I don't know what I'm looking for," said Max.

"Anything related to Project Gemini," Steve said for what seemed like the hundredth time.

Max took off the helmet. "There is nothing more about Project Gemini in there. Alistair is Project Gemini." Max looked closely at Steve for a reaction. If Sergey was right, and Alistair was just the cover for Gemini, it was time for Steve to let him know.

"You already knew about the Project Gemini Overview we found, didn't you?" asked Max.

Max noticed the hint of surprise on Steve's face. Steve paused and rubbed the stubble on his chin. "Yes, Max. I've seen that document before. I didn't tell you because I wanted to see what you would be able to find on your own. To see what kind of access you have. Do you understand?"

Max nodded.

"Alistair couldn't have been all of Project Gemini. I think he was part of it, but just a cover. Too many resources were devoted to the project. There has to be more."

"What do you think it is?" asked Max.

Steve looked at Greg and nodded.

"We think it's highly advanced artificial intelligence Max," said Greg. "You can see hints of it in Alistair. In fact, you were able to activate more than we ever had before, but we think there is much more."

"Why does it matter?"

"That's a great question Max," said Steve. "Artificial intelligence isn't something important in itself; it's what it can do for literally everything that uses a computer chip. It can make interfaces easier to use, diagnose and fix problems, reduce financial fraud, and automate scheduling. It could save us millions of dollars a day in Scientopia alone. But the practical applications are virtually limitless. If we had a viable AI that could interface with other computing systems, Hoff Enterprises would become the most valuable company in the world."

Max saw Steve's eyes glowing with enthusiasm. He had never seen anyone so thoroughly engrossed in a subject. Max looked at Greg, mostly for comfort. Greg nodded his head vigorously. Whatever Steve had, Greg had it too. Max had to speak to break the tension he was feeling.

"Okay. But what is it? What am I looking for?"

"It's code, Max. Computer code. Lines of instructions," said Steve.

Greg intervened. "I think Max has probably had enough for tonight. Let's let him rest and try again next time."

Steve smiled. "You're right. Tell you what Max, why don't we run over to the Galaxy Grill? I could really use a shake."

Both Max and Greg looked at Steve suspiciously.

"I know," said Steve laughing. "I'm supposed to be a vegan. I think even vegans are allowed a little vice now and then. Max, please wait in the lobby. I need to talk to Greg for a minute, and I'll be right out."

Max left.

"What do you think? Have we overestimated him?" asked Steve.

"I don't know. We're asking a lot. He started off so well, but we haven't made any progress. Maybe it's not Max. Maybe there's nothing there," said Greg.

Steve stomped his foot. "No, no, no. There is. There has to be. I know it. You said yourself that no one else is able to use the helmet like Max. The kid has to be the answer. There's no other option."

"What about his meetings with Sergey?" asked Greg.

"We'll let them continue. Sergey may help him find something useful. Be sure and track Max closely," said Steve.

"We can't."

"What do you mean we can't?"

"Just what I said. He's like Sergey, practically invisible to the system. He can go anywhere he wants, and we know nothing about it. It may be something with the biometrics. IT resets his user account each morning, but somehow he still has superuser access. I have several people working on it."

Steve ran his hand through his hair and took a deep breath. He looked like he was getting ready to go on one of his famous rants, but made a visible effort to control himself.

"Greg, we can't have this. With the amount of money I spend on IT it's absurd that we can't lock down the system. Do you know I have to have two computers? One has all of the sensitive documents on it and never connects to the network for fear Sergey will hack it. The other one I use to get access to the Internet and everything else I need. Copy and paste back and forth to a thumb drive for every stupid little thing I want to keep. It's like living in 1985! Now you tell me, we have a billion-dollar tracking system that can't keep tabs on a twelve-year-old kid? I bet Steve Jobs never had to put up with this kind of crap. Make it happen, Greg."

Greg turned to go.

"Oh, and Greg, one more thing. Tell Dieter I'm taking over directly as head of Summer Genius."

"Are you sure that's a good idea? The lab director has been head of the program since it started. He won't like it."

"Am I CEO here or not? What do I care if he likes it? He'll do what I tell him to do or get a new job."

Greg started to speak, paused, then said, "He's been here a long time, Steve. A lot of people look up to him. Might cause problems if you push too far."

Steve seemed to consider the point, but only for a second. "I understand. Go ahead and tell him. This is important."

Steve was all smiles when he joined Max in the lobby. "Let's go. Have you had a shake at the Galaxy Grill yet?"

"Yeah," said Max, grinning.

"I see, you know then what I'm talking about. I'd like to know their secret. I'm CEO, and they won't even tell me, but I've heard there's some cheese in it."

Max scrunched up his face.

"I know; it sounds weird. But you can't argue with success."

They got out of the elevator and walked across the atrium. It was late, but the atrium wasn't completely deserted. Several people couldn't help but watch them as they passed. Steve thought the attention was bothering Max. "That's the price of fame, Max. No privacy - ever. You kind of get used to it, but sometimes, like now, it can be a pain. You know, let's take an APT. That'll be easier."

Steve led the way to the APT station. There was no one in line, and they were able to go right to a car. "Good evening, Steve," said the car. Steve smiled, and Max stepped in behind him. "Good evening, Mr. Hoff," said the car.

Steve's smile vanished. "What was that?" he asked.

Max shrugged. "It's been calling me that ever since I got here. I've told them about it several times, but they haven't been able to fix it. A glitch I guess."

"Just on the cars?"

"No, everywhere," said Max with a slight smile. "It's okay; I don't mind."

Max may not have minded, but Steve did. Why was the system calling Max *Mr. Hoff*? Why did he have untraceable superuser access? Why was Max able to control the helmet so easily? Steve's mind was instantly absorbed with the possibilities, all of which were threatening. In the few minutes it took to get to the Galaxy Grill station, Steve became more determined than ever to find out everything he could about Max. He was twitching with the desire to get back to his computer to run a background check on Max, but in the meantime, he had to satisfy his curiosity the old fashioned way.

"Tell me about your parents, Max."

"It's just my dad and me. Mom died."

"I'm sorry, Max. That must be a hard thing to lose your mother at such a young age."

"Yeah, it was a long time ago."

"What kind of work does your dad do?"

"He has a machine shop. Sometimes he makes parts for Scientopia," Max said with a smile.

"That's great, Max. I'll have to check and see if we can send him more business. We take pride in supporting the Scientopia family."

"My mom used to work here, too."

"Oh, what was her name?"

"Katharine Powers."

Steve struggled to maintain a look of polite interest. His mind was cluttered with confusing thoughts.

"Really? I knew your mother. In fact, I worked closely with her for years. I don't remember her having a child. That's why I never made the connection with the last name."

"I was adopted," said Max softly. "I just found out."

Steve looked up absently for a few seconds. A soft smile radiated from Steve's face.

"I was adopted too, Max. Bet you didn't know that, did you?"

Max shook his head.

"We're lucky, Max. Anyone can love their biological children. Only special people take in strangers as their own. That makes us special, too."

"You finished? I'll take your glass," said Steve as Max slurped the last of his milkshake up the straw. When Steve came back from the counter he had a handful of Hoffpops. He held them out to Max. "What's your favorite flavor?"

Max laughed.

Steve looked confused. "What's funny?"

"It's Alistair. He's always asking people if they want a Hoffpop. They come in seven flavors of sweet, fruity goodness!"

Steve smiled. "He always says those exact words. Have you noticed *when* he does that?"

"When people are sad?"

"That's right. It's in his programming. Alistair is our ambassador. It's his job to make people feel better, to be happy. Whenever he perceives that someone is sad or distressed, he offers them a Hoffpop. Would you like a Hoffpop?"

Max took cherry.

Steve unwrapped a blackberry and popped it into his mouth. He noticed Max looking at him quizzically. "I know, sugar. I'll be better tomorrow. How many licks before you bite it?" Steve crunched his pop to get to the gooey center.

"No willpower," Max said with a grin. Then he bit his pop.

"You're a good kid, Max. Here, let me take that stick." Steve took the stick from Max, wrapped it in a napkin and slid it into his man bag.

The moment passed, and Steve was eager to get back to his office. His mind was swimming with the things he wanted to look up on his computer. He kept looking at his smart watch until, finally, he opened the communicator app. "Alistair, come to the Galaxy Grill and take Max back to his room."

On the way to his office, Steve stopped by the lab. He turned on the lights and went straight to the DNA analyzer. Steve opened his man bag and took out the napkin. He placed Max's Hoffpop stick into the analyzer. While the analyzer did its work, he plugged his thumb drive into the machine's single USB port. When the scan was complete, he pressed the keypad to download the results to the thumb drive. The analyzer beeped when the download was complete. Steve removed the drive, turned off the analyzer and the lights, and continued to his office.

In his office, Steve logged into the laptop that was connected to the network. He paused for a second, aware that if he pulled up only one record he would tip off anyone monitoring his account. He decided that downloading a batch of records would be less suspicious. He thought for a moment, trying to decide what criteria would capture the record he was looking for. An alphabetical range would be too obvious. So would a date range. What about getting all of the corporate officers? That would make sense; he had every reason to do that. Steve wondered if he could search for former officers as well. A bit of fiddling around with the search criteria, and he realized he could. So, that was it. He searched for all corporate officers, past and present, selected all of the results and loaded them onto his thumb drive.

Steve pulled the thumb drive from the network-connected computer and inserted it into the stand-alone computer. He searched through the files he had downloaded until he came to the record he was looking for. Steve then selected Max's profile, paused to take a breath and hit "compare." At first, nothing happened. Steve was beginning to think the computer had frozen when a screen popped up.

"Oh God," Steve said and buried his face in his hands. He could feel his stomach churning. He looked back up, hoping for a mistake, but the results were still there, glowing faintly in the dark office. Steve stared at the screen for a long time. Slowly, he went back to his laptop and hit delete. The message, **Are you sure? This operation cannot be undone** appeared. Steve clicked **OK** and entered his password. **Operation Complete**.

Although Steve's job as visionary didn't require computer expertise, he had learned that digital information had a way of leaking out, even when files had supposedly been deleted. This job was too important to take chances. Steve logged into both his computers and started a reformat of the hard drives. While they were reformatting, he took out the flash drive.

Steve put it on the floor and started pounding it with the crystal Death Star paperweight from his desk. When it was in several pieces, he scooped them up and put them into separate trash cans around the office.

When Steve returned to his desk, each hard drive had been erased and formatted. Steve opened each computer's case, removed the hard drives and placed them in a small sack. *A quick stop at the magnet exhibit should completely wipe these out*, he thought.

Steve took out his phone and texted his assistant to have IT install new hard drives on his computers before morning. He left the office still disturbed at what he'd learned, but pleased at his calm and deliberate efforts to control the damage. All in all, Steve thought as he waited for the elevator, he had done a good job in difficult circumstances.

In the computer room of his lonely split-level house, Sergey Mamontov was preparing to shut down for the night. Despite his love for computers, and years of practice, staring at screens all day took a toll. He rubbed his eyes and decided to do one last thing before logging off.

A few clicks later and Sergey was looking over the virtual shoulder of his one-time associate, the famous visionary, Steve Hunter. As he scrolled through the day's activities, Sergey thought for what must have been the ten-thousandth time how, for a proclaimed visionary, Steve Hunter was boring and self-absorbed. Email after email about what he was to have for lunch, obsessing over the colors of the restroom renovations in the Constellation Theater, and griping with reporters over a story that was scheduled to appear in *Vanity Fair*. Sergey was about to close down when he came to the next to last entry of the day: Steve downloading the full profiles of corporate directors.

That was interesting. Sergey wondered what Steve wanted with those names. While he clicked to another screen, he couldn't help but sneer. Steve, that technological caveman, actually thought that his thumb drive was safe from snooping. Sergey savored the memory of the day he had discovered what Steve was doing with the drive and his stand-alone computer. It had been such a golden opportunity. The virus that he had installed on Steve's thumb drive gave him access to every computer it was plugged into. Thinking he was safe, Steve had become careless and given Sergey access to everything. That was exciting, even if almost everything Steve did was annoyingly dull.

Sergey's self-satisfied smile disappeared as he absorbed what Steve had been reading. *This can't be*, he thought as he clicked deeper. Finally, there it was, in the same glowing text that Steve had seen a few hours earlier. There was no doubt about it, Max was more important to him than ever, and he would have to think very carefully about his next move.

CHAPTER 13

The Summer Geniuses gathered in the classroom before going down to the atrium for the Founders Ball. Max tugged at the sleeves of his sports coat. They were fine as long as he stood still with his arms down, but every time he moved his arms the sleeves rode up.

Normally Max wouldn't have noticed such things, or even cared, but seeing Ryan Fairchild in a tuxedo made him self-conscious. His discomfort increased when he realized that not only Ryan but all the members of Team Turing were wearing tuxes or fancy dresses. Max guessed that Ryan's parents had something to do with it.

He looked around and saw that Hannah was wearing a nice dress, and Jimmy and Aiden had suits that mostly fit right. Looking down at his rumpled khakis, for the first time in his life Max felt the need for an iron. He bent down, deciding if his boat shoes weren't exactly patent leather, they could at least be tied.

"I can tell it's a special occasion, Max if you're tying your shoes."

Max winced, but he knew that Hannah's smile meant she was just teasing.

"I don't have a suit," Max stammered as he stood up.

"It's okay, Max," said Hannah. "You look great. Besides, you're the smartest one here."

Max looked at Hannah sheepishly to see if she was teasing him. To his relief, he decided she wasn't, and he smiled. That made him feel a little better.

"Is your dad coming?" asked Hannah.

Max looked at the floor. "No." Max didn't want to tell Hannah that his dad was no more equipped for a formal ball than he was. He would have liked for his dad to be there, but he understood why that was impossible.

"My dad got a table. You can sit with us."

"Scholars!" said Alistair. "They're ready for us. Line up by teams. One team per lift. When you step out downstairs they'll be introducing you to the crowd. Stand up straight, and be sure to smile. Let's go."

Max fidgeted, waiting for Team Ritchie's turn, relieved not to have to go first, but eager to get it over with, too.

"Here you go, Max!" said Alistair. Alistair looked at Max: "Would you like a Hoffpop? They come in seven flavors of sweet, fruity, goodness."

Max shook his head, mortified at the idea that Alistair could detect his nervousness. Alistair winked, "You're team captain, be sure and step out first. Away you go!"

Max didn't have time to think about how high up he was as the lift descended. All of his thoughts were focused on the crowd below. He hoped he wouldn't do anything stupid. As the lift stopped and the doors opened Max hesitated. After a brief pause he stepped out into the crowd, hoping his teammates were close behind. There was a burst of applause and a few cheers as Max moved forward. He felt like he was in a dream.

Near the end of the path, Max saw Steve and the other teams gathered on a stage at the far end of the atrium. Steve, and everyone on stage was clapping. Max felt his spirits rise. A frightening thought flashed through his mind. What if they asked him to speak in front of the crowd? He quickly pushed the thought away and let himself enjoy the moment.

Max turned to take the stairs to the stage. For an instant, Max thought he was dreaming. Standing right there was his father, clapping, and dressed in a perfect black tuxedo. Their eyes met, and they smiled simultaneously. Max couldn't remember a time when he had been so happy. As he stepped onto the stage he could see the whole crowd, full of people smiling and clapping.

Steve moved to the podium and started speaking. Max didn't hear a thing Steve said. He was too busy enjoying the attention of the crowd.

When Steve finally declared the Founders Ball open, Max immediately moved toward his father. Max was worried about being able to find him in the crowd, but his father was waiting for him at the bottom of the steps.

"Dad! You made it!" Max wanted to give his father a hug, but he thought that might look childish. Max looked up at his father and instantly recognized the worry on his face. "Dad, is everything okay?"

Mr. Powers smiled weakly. "I guess I know why you don't want to give me a hug." Max felt embarrassed at his restraint. "Now that you know I'm not your real father."

Max was horrified. "That's not it at all! I just didn't want to look, you know, like a little kid."

Mr. Power's expression lightened. "Then, you're not ashamed of having me here?"

"Of course not, Dad," Max said. "No matter where I came from, you're still my father. You're the only person I'd ever want to be here with me."

"Nothing was going to keep me away, Max. Not even my old clothes."

Max hugged his father, then released his grip and stepped back, grinning.

"How did you get a tux?"

"It was delivered this afternoon. I guess the park must have sent it. They were probably afraid I was going to show up in my coveralls and ruin their party," Mr. Powers said with a grin.

Max laughed.

"I'm so proud of you Max. The Summer Genius program is a big deal. I hope you've been enjoying it."

"Max!"

Max turned to see Hannah approaching with her father in tow.

"Mr. Powers, you came!" said Hannah.

"How could I miss the chance to see you kids all cleaned up? You look beautiful, Hannah."

Hannah smiled and blushed, her eyes sparkling.

Mr. Powers extended his hand. "It's good to see you again, Mr. Phan."

Hannah's father shook and held on to Mr. Power's hand. "Yes, it is, Mr. Powers. We're all very happy for Max and Hannah. A proud moment to be a father, isn't it?"

Mr. Powers looked at Max, who was displaying a huge grin. "Yes, it is."

"Would you please join us at our table?"

"Thank you, I'm honored," replied Mr. Powers.

Max tugged his father's arm. "Dad, I want you to meet Steve. You too, Mr. Phan."

The quartet made their way back on stage where a group had surrounded Steve. Max noticed Ryan and Kaylee standing together. If that wasn't enough, when Ryan and Kaylee moved closer to Steve, Ryan took a selfie of the trio.

Ryan and Kaylee were lingering nearby when Max got his turn. "Steve, this is my dad, and this is Hannah's dad."

"It's a pleasure to meet you, Tim, and you too, Sam," Steve said shaking each of their hands in turn. "Max and Hannah have been doing great work for us."

Max noticed Ryan and Kaylee listening, and he couldn't help showing off a little. "When's our next session with the helmet, Steve?"

Steve smiled and looked at Max's father. "Yes, Mr. Powers, Max has been helping us with a special project. But Max you need to devote your full attention to the anidroid now, we can take the project from here." Steve winked and stopped talking; leaving no doubt that he was through. Max glanced at Ryan as he was walking away, wondering if Ryan had noticed the slight. The smirk on Ryan's face told Max he had. No doubt Kaylee had too.

On the way to Hannah's table, Max's father observed that Steve seemed odd. "I know," Max muttered.

It soon became apparent to Max that Hannah was intent on making sure he enjoyed himself, even if he resisted. As they returned to their table, the music started, and she pulled him out onto the dance floor. Max had exactly two gym classes worth of square dancing experience which wasn't likely to be helpful. Still, it seemed like a good way to cheer himself up. After observing the other dancers for a minute or so he felt up to shuffling around and jumping up and down a little. Soon his good mood returned. It was hard to be sad with the world's largest disco ball rotating overhead, making everything sparkly.

Max's spirits soared even higher as he recognized the first bars of *Stayin' Alive*. It was one of his dad's favorites, and Max couldn't help but snap his fingers to it.

"Go, Max!" said Hannah.

That was all the encouragement Max needed to do a little spin. When he did, he saw Alistair on the dance floor nearby.

"Hey, look at Alistair," Max said to Hannah.

He and Hannah laughed. Alistair was dancing with Courtney Adams, doing what could only be described as shockingly good John Travolta moves.

"Alistair, I didn't know you could dance!" Max shouted over the music.

"You forget, Max, I am an entertainer!"

Alistair was so entertaining the other dancers stopped and formed a circle to watch. The sudden attention seemed to make Courtney nervous, but Alistair led her through steps that soon had the crowd cheering.

When the song ended, Alistair took Courtney's hand, and they both gave a deep bow. A slow song began, and

Max took Hannah by the hand and led her back to the table. They had only been seated a few seconds when his dad leaned over and whispered that Max should offer to get Hannah a drink. She said she would like a punch, so Max made his way to the punch bowl.

Unfortunately, Ryan and his cronies were standing nearby, as well as a few admirers congratulating him on being at the ball with Kaylee. "Yeah, it's okay," said Ryan.

"What are you going to do afterward?" Justin, from Team McCarthy, asked.

"She's really into me," said Ryan. "Anything could happen," he said, while slowly nodding his head.

The boys laughed.

"What's she really like?" asked Cory, another Team McCarthy guy.

"I don't think she's that smart," said Ryan. "You know, conceited, and silly, too. What do you expect?"

The group had gone quiet while Ryan spoke. Ryan was still bobbing his head, obviously enjoying the attention. One after another the boys followed Justin's gaze as he looked past Ryan.

Max looked, too. There was Kaylee. It was clear from her expression that she had heard what Ryan had said. When Ryan finally turned his head, Max noticed a flicker of discomfort pass across his face, replaced immediately by his regular expression of supreme confidence.

"Hi babe, here's your punch," said Ryan.

Without a word, Kaylee turned and left.

The boys all looked at Ryan. "She'll get over it," he said.

Max's first inclination was to run after Kaylee and console her. Then he remembered the punch, and Hannah, and decided that Kaylee had chosen Ryan and must deal with the consequences herself. Surprisingly, before the end of the next song, Max saw them together as if nothing had happened. For a minute or so Max felt disappointed and confused, but Hannah showed up asking him to say goodbye to her dad, and he left thoughts of Kaylee behind.

Soon after, it was time for Max's father to leave as well.

"Thanks for coming, Dad," said Max.

"I'm glad I did, Max, it was a special night. Are you sure everything's okay? What was that about Steve not needing you for the special project anymore?"

"It's what I told you about before. He wants to find something called Project Gemini, but I don't think we're looking for the right things. Maybe he's right. The helmet didn't help much."

"You can still come home anytime you want."

"No, there's something I need to find. Steve said he knew mom. Did you know that?"

"I don't remember specifically," said Max's dad. "Your mom and I didn't talk about her work much. But she was important here. I had the idea that she knew all of the top people."

"Did she ever say anything about Project Gemini?"

"I don't remember," said his father. "All I know is that they terminated the project she was working on when Mr. Hoff died. It might have been that project."

"Can you see if there's anything at home that might help?"

"There's not much, but I'll look. What is it I'm looking for?"

"I don't know. Anything that looks like it may be related to Project Gemini."

After he was ready for bed, Max, as he often did, logged onto Roblox to play a few games and chat with his friends. He hadn't been on long when he heard the distinctive sound of an incoming Skype call. Max minimized his browser and saw that his dad was calling.

"Hey, Dad."

"Max, are you all right?" Max noticed right away his dad seemed agitated.

"Yeah, I'm okay. Just checking on Roblox."

"Has anything happened there?" his dad said quickly.

"No. What's wrong?"

"Someone's been in the house. They turned it upside down." His dad moved aside and turned the camera so that Max could see the room. Drawers were pulled out, cushions overturned, and things thrown all over the floor.

"Is anything gone?"

"Not that I can tell," answered his father.

"Why do you think it had anything to do with me?"

"Because I'm always home in the evening. Only the people at Scientopia knew I would be out tonight."

After Max finished talking with his dad and shut down his computer, he lay awake in bed for a long time, thinking about what had happened that day. Why had Steve so abruptly ended the project? Who had sent his dad a tux? Why had his house been robbed? Max felt like there must be something he was missing, something that would tie together all these questions together. Just before falling asleep, he thought of one more question, unrelated but troubling. *Why had Kaylee gone back to Ryan after the terrible things he said?*

CHAPTER 14

The Founders Ball was over. The last guests were gone and the rigging crew was breaking down the stage. In Steve's office at the top of the Crystal Tower, Dieter Lehrer, Greg Symonds, and Steve Hunter stood together. Steve's loosened tie dangled, and his collar was open. He kicked his shoes off and stood in his rainbow-colored socks.

"You can't do it, Steve," Lehrer said, drawing out Steve's name.

Lehrer; the rigid, scientific German, got under his skin.

"Can't do what? I'm CEO."

"Replace me as director of the Summer Genius program," replied Dieter. "You don't have the support."

Steve looked at Greg, who didn't move. Steve took that as a bad sign.

"Okay, tell you what, Dieter. Let the kid go, and you can keep your position," said Steve. He dropped onto the couch carelessly and spread out in a move calculated to appear confident and unconcerned.

"Why do you want to get rid of Max?" Dieter asked.

"He has violated several policies," answered Steve.

"Which ones?"

"It's a privacy issue. I am not at liberty to say," said Steve.

"Pfft. I'm the head of the program. I should know about any violations. There is no privacy issue," said Dieter.

"There will be if I dismiss you."

"Why don't you?" said Dieter. "Tell him Symonds. Let Steve know what will happen if he tries to dismiss me."

Steve locked eyes with Greg Symonds, who didn't say anything. "Go ahead Greg," said Steve. "What is he talking about?"

"The engineering staff will walk out," said Greg.

"How many?" asked Steve.

"Practically everyone…" Greg said.

"Go ahead," said Steve.

"There's a rumor that Disney is ready to hire the whole department."

Dieter remained impassive, but Steve thought he saw a hint of triumph in his eyes. The thought enraged him.

"Why are you willing to go to the mat over this kid?" asked Steve.

"That is not important," said Dieter. "The interesting question is why are you? He's just an insignificant boy whose greatest challenge each day is getting his shoes tied. Why would you even care if he's in the program or not?"

Steve almost lost his temper. He resisted the impulse because he didn't think it would work with Dieter, and he didn't want to give him the satisfaction. Steve decided to go with a reasoned, but passionate attack. "You just don't get it do you, Dieter? This park is in serious trouble. Do you ever bother to look at attendance figures? Has your lab developed a single breakthrough technology in the last five years? I'm doing everything I can to save this place, and I would appreciate your help."

Steve didn't expect Dieter's laughter or his response. "Do you think I am a child?" said Dieter. "Or perhaps one of your silly, young marketing people? How does saving the park have anything to do with Max Powers? It seems to me, Steve, that there is something you are not telling me."

Steve heard the contempt in Dieter's voice. This was clearly going nowhere. Dieter was less moveable than the Alps. He needed to approach this from a different direction. Steve looked away and took a deep breath, ordering his thoughts.

Steve turned back to Dieter. "No. Dieter, you are right. This is a stupid waste of time on my part. Max's transgressions are minor compared with many things that have happened in years past. He will stay, and I hope you will, too. Scientopia needs your knowledge and experience."

"Yes, yes of course," said Dieter before turning to leave.

Steve was still on the couch, looking glum. Greg waited until Dieter was gone before speaking: "Why do you want to get rid of Max? Don't we need him to help find Gemini?"

"You saw how it was going. We weren't making any progress. We don't need the kid."

"I don't see how it could hurt to give him more time. He's better with the helmet than anyone else. Isn't Gemini important?"

Steve sighed. Frustration was welling up inside of him. He hated being questioned, but he needed to keep Greg on his side. "Gemini is more important than ever. It may be the thing that saves us. I know Hoff was close. If we can find it, I'm sure we could turn things around. But it has to be without Max."

"Because of his connection with Sergey?" Greg asked.

Steve smiled inwardly. There it was on a platter, the excuse to push Max out that he'd been seeking. Steve wondered for a second why he hadn't thought of it earlier, but he quickly dismissed the thought. He was a visionary. His primary skill was the ability to recognize others' good ideas.

"That's right, Greg. We can't trust Max. He's too close to Sergey. We can't take the risk."

"Yeah, you're right," said Greg. "I see now what you've been thinking. I should have realized sooner. Max needs to go."

Max was rushing to the Restaurant at the End of the Universe to meet Jimmy and Aiden for lunch. He had lingered in the lab to finish compiling the latest version of the droid's operating system, but he didn't want to miss the dinosaur fingers that Aiden had been raving about.

"Max."

Max looked around but didn't see anyone, just a park alien.

"Max, in here, it's me." The alien lifted up its elongated foam head. Inside was Sergey.

"Is this an alien abduction?" asked Max.

"Don't be ridiculous, Max. We have to talk before they find me."

"And this won't be suspicious?" asked Max, rolling his eyes.

"It seemed like a good idea at the time. They're on to me. I have to keep changing my disguises."

"Why don't you try Evil Genius?" said Max.

"Very funny. Let's step beside this building," said Sergey.

They stepped to the side of a kiosk selling nebula clouds, which looked a lot like cotton candy.

"How's it going?" asked Sergey.

"Steve ended the project," said Max.

"I figured he would."

"Why?"

"You were getting too close. It was making him nervous."

"Why would it make him nervous?" asked Max. "I thought he wanted to find Project Gemini?"

"He does, but he wants to be the one to find it. You probably showed him what he needs to finish the job," said Sergey.

Max looked at Sergey suspiciously. It was bad enough to be talking to a foam alien. For the conversation to be about conspiracy theories too was just a bit much.

"What would it matter to him if I found it? It's not like I could do anything with it. He's the CEO. I'm just a kid."

"You don't understand people like Steve, Max. You and I are alike. We want to learn, to create. Steve just wants to be in control and make himself more important." Does that make sense?"

"Yeah, I guess."

"Here, I have something to help you." Sergey tried to hand Max a thumb drive that was on a lanyard around his neck, but he couldn't get it over the huge foam head. After trying to break the string, Sergey said, "crap," lifted the alien head up, took the lanyard off, and put the head back on.

"What is it?" said Max.

"It's an emulator. It virtualizes all of the information on the park's network. It will allow you to get out of the library and see everything else. Just plug it into whatever computer the helmet is connected to."

"I don't get it," said Max.

"Max, everything is information. Look around you here. All that you see, the whole universe, could be a part of a big computer simulation. It's the same with the information stored in the cloud. It can be represented visually. This program allows that."

"What will I be looking for? Steve said I'm supposed to be looking for computer code."

"Project Gemini is a chip, Max. Steve's an idiot. There's no code; it's just a chip. An optical chip. It looks like a crystal. You'll know it when you find it."

"Why can't you do it?" asked Max.

"Because you have better access than I do. I don't know why but you do," said Sergey.

Max looked into Sergey's big alien eyes. "This is getting too hard," Max said and looked at the ground. "I don't know if I can keep this up. I don't know what I'm doing."

"Max, everyone else knows even less. You're the only one in the world who can bring back Project Gemini."

"Why should I care?" asked Max.

"Because your mother did. Project Gemini was her life's work. Verner thought this was so important that he trusted only her to see this project through. Your mother can't finish the job Max, but you can."

"Why do you care?"

"Because what I created was taken from me. I want it back to save Scientopia and make a difference in the real world. This will be a change as big as the invention of the computer itself. Don't you want to be a part of that, Max?"

Max didn't say anything. It made sense, but it seemed like it would be hard too. "Someone broke into our house. Did you do that?"

"Max, why would I do that? Have I lied to you? Steve is the one who deceived you isn't he?"

Max nodded.

"You need to decide. Are you going to let your mother down, Max?"

Max shook his head and whispered, "No."

"We're going to finish this?" asked Sergey.

"Yeah," Max said as he turned to walk away.

"Max."

Max looked back.

"Be careful. There's no telling what Steve might do to you."

CHAPTER 15

Max inspected the four ani-droids lined up in the front of the class for the mid-term evaluation. The familiar nut of nervousness in his stomach was feeling more like a watermelon.

He wasn't worried about the work done by Team McCarthy and Team Shannon. Team McCarthy had decided to mirror Scientopia's space theme and build an astronaut. They named him Buck. Unfortunately, they had been unable to find a spacesuit. They improvised with tubing that gave the strong impression of a man who'd gotten his head stuck in a fishbowl after being swallowed by a vacuum cleaner hose.

Team Shannon, on the other hand, had been torn by an argument over whether their ani-droid should look like a Transformer or a Wookiee. When they were told that neither option was acceptable, since Scientopia didn't own the rights to either, they decided to mix and match parts from both. The resulting mutant was really beyond description, though someone thought it looked like a wooly mammoth that had strayed in front of a harvester.

It was Team Turing that had Max worried. Their ani-droid was big, dark and intimidating. Its bulging black plastic muscles filled the room like a Greek statue. Standing tall and erect, it had an unmistakable military air that made it seem more like a member of Navy Seal Team Six than Summer Genius Team Turing.

Finally, there was the Team Ritchie ani-droid, the one put together by Max and his teammates. It had seemed like such a good decision to model their ani-droid on Alistair. Everyone liked cuddly Alistair. He was proven, approachable, without risk. A sure bet.

And not the least bit impressive.

Barely taller than Max, with a big bald head, a torso too small, and legs too short, the Team Ritchie ani-droid, which they had named Dexter, was everything an actual human shouldn't be. Comparing Dexter to Rob, the Team Turing ani-droid, was like comparing Elmo to Optimus Prime. In a battle, he wouldn't stand a chance.

Sitting in his seat, waiting for the evaluation to get started, Max knew how it felt to be defeated before the battle had begun.

His teammates' felt it, too. Even Hannah, always-optimistic Hannah, had said second place wouldn't be so bad. Max silently agreed with her. Who would bet on Mickey Mouse against Ironman?

Losing was bad enough. Losing to Ryan was worse than bad. Max could sense his gloating from across the room. This contest was becoming about more than a couple of ani-droids; it was personal. Ryan, all blonde and confident, had all the polish a person could want. Max couldn't compete with Ryan in certain categories, but he had real brains and ability. Max had always banked on the thought that, when it mattered, his ingenuity would help him come out on top.

If Ryan's charm was paired with superior performance, Max was doomed. Attractive and dull he could handle, attractive and smart was too much. He felt like giving up before the evaluation had even begun.

Alistair called the room to order, and Dr. Lehrer began immediately.

"This will be an informal process," said Lehrer. "Dr. Symonds and I are looking for progress and understanding. We will offer suggestions, and you may ask questions. We will start with Team Turing. Rob, how are you doing today?"

"I'm fine, thank you, how are you?" the Team Turing ani-droid answered.

"Rob, I am lost, how do I get to the Galaxy Grill?" asked Lehrer.

There was a long pause before Rob responded with flawless directions.

"Rob, bring me the eraser on the white board."

There were two whiteboards at the front of the room, each with an eraser resting in the tray. Rob turned his head, located the one closest to him and moved toward it. Before reaching the first board, he stopped. He moved his head toward the second board and back toward the first.

"Rob, bring me the eraser closest to you," said Dr. Lehrer.

It was no use; Rob was in a loop. "Rob, stop," said Lehrer.

Nothing changed. Rob remained in place looking first at one eraser and then the other.

"Rob, discontinue. Rob, return. Rob, shut down." Dr. Lehrer gave strings of orders without any change in the ani-droid's behavior.

"Mr. Ryan, please disable your ani-droid," said Dr. Lehrer.

"Rob, stop," said Ryan.

Rob stopped moving his head immediately. Ryan ordered him to return to his position, and he did.

"Well, Team Turing, you have done an extraordinary job with the look of your ani-droid. Your focus now should obviously be on the control systems. Don't be discouraged, you have done very well, this is what we expect at this stage of the competition."

Dr. Lehrer was about to move on to the Team McCarthy ani-droid when he paused.

"This brings up an important point. Perhaps you noticed how Rob didn't stop when I ordered him to, but he did for Mr. Fairchild. Who is in charge of these ani-droids? Can just anyone issue an order and expect it to be obeyed? What if Rob was walking through the park, and a guest gave him and order, what should he do? It may not matter if the order was something simple, but what would happen if the order was harmful and the ani-droid obeyed? How could we control for this problem? Should only certain people be able to give orders, or should the ani-droid be autonomous, following any order it thinks is valid?"

Dr. Lehrer paused and crossed his arms. He rubbed his forehead before continuing, "This can become a very complicated subject, especially since our ani-droids at Scientopia interact with the general public. You must be careful to copy Alistair's permissions and protection module into your machines. It works very well, and we shouldn't be wasting time recreating things that are already proven."

Dr. Lehrer continued his examination of the ani-droids. Though it looked silly, Team McCarthy's spaceman did everything asked with only minor glitches. Team Shannon wasn't so fortunate. Their ani-droid, which was named Chewformer, wouldn't power up. Max could hear the team's whispered recriminations start before Lehrer had even delivered his verdict.

"That will be enough, Team Shannon," said Dr. Lehrer. You clearly have work to do. I will meet will all of you after class. Now, let's move on to Team Ritchie. Hello Dexter, how are you?"

Max had noticed that Dexter had been moving his head about during the previous examinations as if taking it all in. He was afraid Dexter had fallen into a loop and wouldn't be able to recover.

"I am most excellent, sir, it's a beautiful day at Scientopia. What can I do for you?" Dexter replied in a chipper voice.

"Dexter, I am lost, could you please tell me how to get to the Galaxy Grill?"

"With pleasure. Would you like to walk or take an APT? It's a 15-minute walk, about the same by APT this time of day, but it sure saves the shoe leather."

"The APT sounds nice, how do I do that?"

Dexter gave directions and made sure Lehrer understood them. Dr. Lehrer smiled.

"Dexter, please bring me the eraser on the white board."

Without looking, Dexter asked, "Do you care which one?"

Max had no idea how he did that, Drs. Lehrer and Symonds seemed impressed too. Once Dexter had picked up the eraser and was bringing it to Lehrer, Symonds threw in a wrinkle.

"Dexter, would you bring the eraser to me instead?"

"I'm sorry, Dr. Symonds, you'll have to wait your turn; this eraser is for Dr. Lehrer."

"You can give the eraser to Dr. Symonds, Dexter," said Dr. Lehrer.

Dexter handed the eraser to Dr. Symonds. Dr. Lehrer started to clap. Dr. Symonds quickly joined him, followed by the whole class.

"Very well done Team Ritchie. I think that is the best mid-term evaluation I have ever seen. How did you get Dexter to offer us options?"

"We just used Alistair's code base," said Max.

"But didn't the other teams use the same?" asked Dr. Lehrer as he looked to the other teams for confirmation.

"We took the code base directly from Alistair," said Max. "Not the original network copy. He has all sorts of experience that makes him work better."

"Of course," said Dr. Lehrer. "A very good point. You were smart to realize that."

"How did he know me?" asked Dr. Symonds. "Alistair doesn't store biometrics."

Max smiled. That had been his idea. "We put a RFID reader in an empty port. It reads the chip in your ID card."

"How did you decide on the look?" asked Dr. Symonds. "He's very...approachable."

Max nodded to Hannah. She had been the strongest advocate for making Dexter similar to Alistair. Hannah answered, "Since we had a model and parts we could put him together more quickly. That was our first reason. We also decided that since he would be working with little kids and families, he should be friendly."

Dr. Symonds nodded his head in agreement. "That's a good point, Hannah. The equipment we make should fit the task. I think Dexter would fit in very well at Scientopia."

Dr. Lehrer stood up. "Well, scholars, it's clear that Team Ritchie is setting the standard. You will all have to work hard to surpass them in the final competition. Take your ani-droids back to your lab stations and get started. Team Shannon see me over here please."

As the class broke up, and Max and his teammates were chattering over their success, Max saw Ryan staring at him from across the room. The look of superiority had vanished, replaced with a cold glare. It wasn't a big jump for Max to realize that meant trouble.

CHAPTER 16

When Max, Hannah, and the rest of Team Ritchie returned to their lab station, they sat Dexter on the edge of what they called the operating table. It was just a lab cart on wheels, but calling it an operating table made it feel more like they were doing serious work. Jimmy plugged Dexter in, and they all started talking at once about what their next steps should be. Aiden was pushing hard to install a jetpack, a topic he wouldn't let go after seeing the jetpack demonstration in the Kennedy Amphitheater yesterday.

"Aiden that's just ridiculous," said Hannah. "What possible use could a jetpack have? You heard Greg. We should build Dexter to fit the task, and I don't see how flying around with a jetpack is useful."

"You're too serious, Hannah," said Aiden. "It would be cool. And fun. This *is* an amusement park, you know."

Max wished everything could be settled with logic, but it never seemed to work out that way. More often, those in disagreement would beat each other over the head with partially-reasoned points and emotional appeals until someone gave in. He wondered if the world outside the lab worked that way, too.

Max noticed Alistair hovering at the edge of the lab. Partly to get away from his arguing teammates, and partly to see Alistair's reaction to the morning's evaluation, Max approached his mechanical friend.

"Hi, Alistair," said Max.

"Hello, Max," said Alistair.

"What did you think of the evaluation?"

"As you know, Max, I don't think. I simply process information."

That seemed, to Max, a testy response for Alistair.

"How did you process the results then?"

"Team Ritchie did very well, Max. Dr. Lehrer said so. He would know better than me."

"Is there something wrong, Alistair?"

"You have done nothing wrong, Max. I have considered whether it is a breach of human etiquette to take the thoughts of one person and put them in another, but I don't have enough information."

"What do you mean, Alistair?"

"You took my data and loaded it into Dexter. I did not know you were going to do that."

"Oh," said Max. "I didn't think it would be a problem."

"Because I am not a person?"

"Yeah. And because, well, it was just data."

"Are your thoughts more than just data, Max?"

"I don't know. Maybe. I still don't see why it matters, Alistair. Isn't transferring your data into Dexter kind of like a parent passing DNA on to their children?"

Alistair moved his head in something that looked like surprise. "I hadn't processed it like that Max. So, my mother put data into me, and I added my experiences and passed it on to Dexter?"

Max giggled. "You have a mother?"

"Yes, my project manager, Katharine Powers. She is listed in my specifications sheet as my mother. It may have been a joke."

Max was shocked at the mention of his mother's name.

"Is anything wrong, Max?"

"Katharine Powers...she's my mother."

"I wasn't aware you had a mother. It's not in your records."

"Everyone has a mother, Alistair," Max smiled broadly. "And it looks like you do as well."

Alistair paused and looked at Max as if he was thinking. "Then we are brothers, are we not, Max?"

Max chuckled. "Yeah. I guess so."

"And passing on my data to Dexter makes me a father, too?"

"That makes sense. We have a bigger family than we thought, Alistair. I wonder what dad is going to think about this."

From the crack under the door, Max could tell that the lights in Hannah's room were off. He pushed it open. "Are you awake?" With only a sliver of light from the hall to show the way, Max crept to the side of Hannah's bed and poked her shoulder. "Wake up."

Hannah stirred. "Max, what are you doing? How'd you get in here?" As her head cleared, "What do you want?"

"I need your help."

"With what?"

"To get the helmet. Sergey gave me a drive with a program on it. It should help us find Gemini."

"That's not a good idea, Max. We might get caught. Wait until morning to tell Steve."

"I don't trust Steve."

Hannah didn't say anything.

"Never mind," said Max. "I can do it myself."

"No wait, I'm coming," said Hannah as she got out of bed. "Wait outside. I need to change."

Max blinked at the bright lights as he went back into the hall. Hannah joined him a couple of minutes later. Hannah had the gift of getting ready quickly, and she had saved more time by doing nothing with her hair, which was sticking up in every possible direction. She saw Max looking at it. "Do you want me to come or not."

"Yeah. It's okay. Let's go." They started down the hall toward the elevator.

"Where are we going?" Hannah asked.

"Steve's office."

Hannah exhaled loudly. "We better not get caught there."

It felt weird walking the empty halls of the Death Star. Half the lights were turned out for the night, but it wasn't dark enough to hide them if someone else was in the building.

"We could sure use an invisibility cloak right about now," said Hannah.

"Yeah, well at least we don't have ghosts wandering all over like at Hogwarts," said Max.

"I was never much into magic," said Hannah.

"Me either," said Max.

"You know they are working on an invisibility cloak," said Hannah. "It works by fiber optics taking the light from behind and guiding it to the front, kind of like a screen."

"Hannah, not now," said Max. Best friend or not, Max did sometimes wish for a switch to stop her chatter.

The elevator door opened. The chime announcing the car's arrival sounded like an alarm in the empty hallway. Max stepped out of the elevator and was relieved to see that the lighting level was much lower up here. There were no overhead lights on, only a few along the wall that put out just enough power for them to be able to make their way around.

"What's that?" whispered Hannah nervously.

Max heard it, too. Footsteps coming towards them, but they couldn't tell from which direction. Max listened a second and said, "This way." He led Hannah down the hall trying to move quickly and quietly. They ducked into the only door on the hall. It was the men's restroom.

"Eww, I can't be in here," said Hannah.

Max rolled his eyes. "There's no one here. Come on," Max said, leading Hannah to the stalls.

"What are those?" she asked pointing towards the urinals.

"Really?"

"How should I know?"

Max opened the door to the third stall. "In here."

"What are we doing?"

Max didn't answer. He stepped up on the toilet, reached for Hannah and shifted back to make room for her to step up. He looked at the stall door and thought about closing it, but decided leaving it cracked open looked more natural.

He heard the door to the hall open and footsteps as someone walked in. "Anybody here?" a male voice said.

Max could feel his heart pounding and Hannah's where she was pressed against him. They both seemed to be beating hard enough to make noise.

The footsteps came closer. Max heard the door to the first stall creak as the man pushed it open. The man stepped to the second door and opened it too. The man moved towards their stall. Max caught a glimpse of him through the crack at the door hinge. He was wearing a uniform. It was a park security guard.

Max braced himself, waiting for the door to their stall to open. Instead, Max saw the guard lean down. He was checking for feet in the last two stalls.

Satisfied, the guard walked away, turning the lights out before leaving. Max and Hannah perched on the toilet in complete darkness, trying not to breathe.

Max couldn't tell how long they remained there before it seemed safe to move. The darkness made it difficult to gauge the passage of time. The blackness was so complete that they both had to move carefully.

"What are we going to do?" Hannah whispered.

"Keep going," said Max.

"What about the guard? We're sure to get caught."

"We just have to be careful."

119

"Can't you, you know, do your special thing? Maybe you can see where he is or how to get around him."

"That's a good idea." Max closed his eyes and focused on retrieving anything related to this floor of the Crystal Tower.

"Yeah, I can see the map of this floor. Hang on." Max concentrated on the security system. Several points lit up on the map with a series of numbers. "It looks like the guard has several checkpoints he goes to on his rounds."

"Can we get by?"

"Not now, but he's got one more stop on this floor, and then a floor below us. That'll give us plenty of time. Let's get to the door."

Max took Hannah's hand and felt his way to the restroom door. When he heard the guard's footsteps going down the stairs, he opened the door and crept into the hall, pulling Hannah behind him.

They scurried down the hall moving as quickly and quietly as they could. They turned the corner and ran a few more steps to the glass doors of Steve's office. Max grabbed the handle, closed his eyes for a second in silent prayer and pulled.

It wouldn't open. The door was locked.

Max opened his eyes and looked around in panic.

"A keypad!" said Hannah pointing to the wall beside the door. "Hurry, I think he's coming back."

Max stepped to the keypad and closed his eyes once again, this time concentrating, and hoping for guidance. The first image that flashed into his mind was the map of the floor. It was showing that the guard was on his way back. *Concentrate,* he said to himself. He put his hand to the keypad. His fingers started pressing the numbers: **23564**. Max held his breath for an instant, not knowing whether they would get in, or if an alarm would sound, or if the floor would open up and swallow them.

The electronic lock made a distinct *click.*

Hannah was already pushing it open.

They could hear the guard approaching. Max stepped through behind Hannah and pushed against the door, hoping it would close faster. After what seemed like a hundred years, it closed with a dull thud that Max knew the guard would hear. They ducked behind the reception desk beside the door. A second later they heard the guard trying to open the door. The lock held and the guard continued on his rounds. Max and Hannah leaned back against the desk, waiting for their racing hearts to slow down.

"Now what?" asked Hannah.

"Come on. The helmet is in the loft," said Max, hoping it was still there.

At the top of the stairs, Max sighed with relief. The helmet right where he left it.

"Do you know how to use it?" asked Hannah.

"I think so. Turn on the computer."

The login screen came up, and Max quickly typed in his username and password. The computer beeped and flashed the message "Access Denied."

"Crap," said Max. "I typed in my password."

Max closed his eyes to concentrate. His fingers flew over the keyboard. The computer hesitated, then the login screen disappeared.

"We're in," said Max.

Max opened the helmet controller. The helmet status light began to glow.

"You stand here," Max said to Hannah. "If this download graph spikes or if I scream or pass out, hit the disconnect key. If that doesn't work, yank the cords out of the helmet. Can you do that?"

Hannah hesitated. Finally, she said, "I think so."

Max flashed Hannah a weak smile as he lifted the helmet to his head. "We have this nailed," he said before disappearing into the helmet.

It took Max a second to orient himself. For a brief moment he was afraid he wouldn't be able to make it work.

"Now?" Hannah asked.

"No. I got it." Max forced himself to relax. The panic began to ebb, and he was suddenly back in the virtual library.

"I'm fine." Max said, trying to reassure himself and Hannah at the same time.

Max looked around the library. He was disappointed to see that it looked exactly as it had before. Something wasn't right.

"Wait a minute." Max fished into his pocket and pulled out a thumb drive. Blinded by the helmet he held his hand straight out. "Here. Put this in the USB drive," he said to Hannah.

"Do we have to shut down first?"

"I don't think so, just do it."

The computer took a few seconds to mount the drive. Nothing changed.

"Do I have to do anything else?" asked Hannah.

"I don't think so," said Max.

Suddenly Max's field of vision was filled with an intense white light. It was as if he had been in a dark room and someone turned on the world's brightest bulb. He closed his eyes, but that didn't help. The explosion of light was in his mind.

Nine miles away, in Sergey's disheveled split-level, an alarm sounded. He clicked the flashing icon to open the alert window. He smiled. *The little bastard is in.*

"What should I do?" said Hannah.

The flash faded as quickly as it had appeared. "Nothing. I'm okay."

Max could see the library again. This time, it was different. In addition to shelves lined with virtual books, there were doors that he had not seen before. Some were labeled, others weren't.

Max looked around trying to decide where to go. The closest door was labeled **Rides**. He opened it and saw a semicircular room full of doors, each marked with the name of one of Scientopia's rides. Max stepped inside and opened the closest door on the right, labeled *Cyclone*. For a second he was confused. The room was black except for a box with a glowing red light. As Max moved closer, he could see that there was a switch in the **Off** position.

"Oh yeah," he said aloud.

"What? What do you see?" exclaimed Hannah.

"The rides. But they aren't doing anything because the park is closed."

Hannah huffed. "Would you quit fooling around and find what we're looking for? Hey, what are we looking for?"

Max stepped back into the library. "I don't know yet." He scanned the labels on the doors for some clue or suggestion as to what he should do next.

He was immediately drawn to the door marked **Restricted Access**. He stepped through and found a room full of filing cabinets. He quickly moved from one cabinet to another reading the labels. There was a cabinet for **Competition Reports**, another for **Employee Availability Outlook**, and another labeled **Addictive Behaviors**. Max wanted to find out why there was a cabinet labeled **Addictive Behaviors** but he had to focus on Project Gemini. After a few minutes, he found a label for **Closed Projects**.

The second drawer was labeled **G-K**. Max pulled it open. The third file folder from the front was labeled **Gemini**.

Max was so excited his concentration began to wane. The file became transparent and started to fade. Focusing once again, Max pulled the folder out of the drawer and opened it. It was stuffed with papers.

The first sheet was a title page. Centered at the top was **Project Gemini**. Closer to the bottom in smaller type was the name **Katharine Powers** and under that **Program Manager**. The Hoff Enterprises logo appeared at the very bottom.

Max eagerly turned the page. The second page had a single word in all caps across the middle: **Deleted**. Max turned to the next page and the one after that. They both contained a single word:**Deleted**. Max quickly shuffled through the remaining pages and all they contained was the word **Deleted**. Max sighed loudly. It was a total dead end.

"What is it Max?" asked Hannah.

"It's all gone. There's nothing here. Someone deleted it."

"Who?"

"It doesn't say."

Wait a minute. Computers do keep a record of deletions. He just had to find it. Max described everything he saw to Hannah.

"Look on the inside cover of the folder," said Hannah. "That would make sense."

Max laid the papers aside to look more closely at the folder. There it was, in small Helvetica type; the name of each file with the notation **Deleted by s_hunter**.

It made no sense that Steve was the one who deleted the files. Wasn't he looking for them? What was going on?

"Did you find anything?" asked Hannah.

"Yeah. It was Steve. Steve Hunter deleted the files."

"When?" asked Hannah.

Max looked at the timestamp on each entry. "Twelve years ago."

Max pulled the helmet off.

"Why would he do that?" asked Hannah. "What does it mean?"

"I don't know, but we'd better get out of here. Maybe Sergey will know."

Max and Hannah shut down the computer and put everything back where they found it. They hurried down the steps from the loft and headed towards the door. As they entered the reception area, Max heard voices from the corridor. He pulled Hannah behind the partition at the edge of the reception area. One of the voices said, "There was an unauthorized login attempt from one of Steve's computers. We need to check it out."

Max heard them fumbling with the lock. They were coming in.

Max quickly scanned the large, dimly lit office. It took him about a second to realize there was only one option. "Up here," he whispered before leading Hannah up the stairs to the catwalk. They opened the door and went outside. He heard the door close with a *click*. They laid down behind a gray panel so that no one inside could see them.

They lay there for what seemed like a long time until Max found the courage to peek over the panel. He saw the security guard standing by while another man was checking the computers.

After another thirty minutes Max looked up again. The office was empty. "I think we can leave now," said Max. Hannah didn't respond. "Hannah? Hannah, wake up."

Hannah raised here head. "Where are we?" she asked sleepily.

"They're gone. We can go now," said Max.

"Oh, yeah."

They both stood. Max pulled on the door. It didn't budge. He pulled on it a few more times. "It's locked," he said. "Is there another door?"

"No," said Hannah. She shivered. It was cold way up there in the dark.

Max sat down with his back against the door. Hannah sat down beside him. He was starting to feel tired, but he was too full of dread to fall asleep.

"We're screwed," said Hannah as she rested her head on his shoulder.

"Yeah," was the last thing Max remembered saying.

CHAPTER 17

The sound of the door opening woke Max. It was still dark, and he had no idea what time it was. He nudged Hannah.

"Wake up." Hannah opened her eyes and froze when she saw that they were still stuck out on the catwalk, far above the park.

Max turned back to see who was coming through the door. He thought his heart was going to leap out of his chest.

It was Alistair.

Alistair scanned both of them and smiled.

"Kind of late to be sightseeing isn't it kids? Come on. We need to get you back to your rooms."

"How did you know we were here?" asked Max once they were back inside.

"You and I, we know things don't we Max?" replied Alistair.

"Yeah, I guess we do," said Max.

The three entered the building, which was still deserted. Alistair's silence was a clue that Max and Hannah needed to be quiet as well. Once they were on the elevator back down to the ground floor, Alistair turned to Max.

"Was it worth it?" asked Alistair.

"Yes, yes it was," said Max.

Max often found the chatter in the lab annoying. This was one of those times. He was trying to sort out how to have Alistair's AI routines run on Dexter's limited processor and Joey Nguyen wouldn't stop yakking with Hannah.

Joey was on Team Turing. Why was he spending so much time in the Team Ritchie lab bay? Max had toyed with the idea that Joey was a spy. He'd decided that if

Joey *was* a spy he wasn't a very good one. Joey never asked questions about what they were doing and didn't seem to understand the programming, which was about the only thing that mattered at this point since all of the mechanics were working as well as could be expected.

Max glanced at Hannah and Joey, oblivious to how annoying they could be. The thought crossed Max's mind once again that Joey was far more interested in Hannah than ani-droids. Joey went out of his way to come over and talk to her. Sometimes he made her laugh. That couldn't be an accident. Hannah did nothing to discourage him, or anyone else, who would listen to her.

Something Joey said caught Max's attention. Max replayed the last minute or so in his mind and realized that Joey had mentioned something Team Turing had done to speed up their droid. Something that didn't seem right.

Max turned to Joey and asked, "What did you say?"

Hannah and Joey looked at Max with mild surprise on their faces.

"What, Max?" asked Hannah.

"Joey. What was Joey saying they had done to Rob?"

"I don't understand it exactly," said Joey. "Ryan discovered that Rob's computer controller was constantly calling routines that were slowing him down. He deleted the calls and now Rob is running much faster." Joey's face registered alarm. "Hey, you're not going to use that against us, are you?"

Max ignored the question and asked, "Which routines did you eliminate?"

Joey looked nervously at the floor and said nothing.

Max wondered which routines Ryan could have eliminated. He had a strong suspicion that it was the protection program. He couldn't think of anything else that could be deleted without affecting the ani-droid's operation. All of the other big processor drains were for sensors that had to keep working. But surely Ryan wouldn't do anything so stupid, especially after what Dieter said.

Hannah and Joey resumed their conversation, but Max was able to tune them out completely as he decided what to do. If Joey was right, Ryan and Team Turing were creating a potentially dangerous ani-droid. If something went wrong, and Max had knowledge that could have stopped it...that wouldn't be good. Max made a decision and stood up.

"Where are you going, Max?" asked Hannah.

Max didn't answer. He had Ryan in his sights in the next lab, and he was going to confront him.

Ryan saw Max coming: "Hey Maxie, coming over to Team Turing to see how things are done? Sorry, can't help."

Max ignored the taunts. "Which routines have you eliminated?" asked Max.

Ryan didn't blink or show any surprise. "What makes you think we've eliminated any routines?"

Max nodded his head in the direction of Joey, still engrossed in his conversation with Hannah.

Ryan smirked. "I should have known. Joey doesn't really fit in here anyway. Seems like he would rather be with the losers."

"Was he right?" asked Max.

"Joey doesn't know what he's talking about," said Ryan. The other Team Turing members were now paying attention to the conversation.

Rather than being intimidated by Ryan, or the attention of the others, Max was starting to feel powerful. "Maybe he doesn't, but have you eliminated routines in Rob's controller?" Max was surprised at how forceful his question came out.

"And what if we did? It's no business of yours," said Ryan.

"That's right," Neil chimed in.

"It is if those were the protection routines. You heard Dr. Lehrer," said Max. "Without the protection routines, it's not safe to have ani-droids around people."

"Cool your jets, Maxie," said Ryan. "The routines are still there. We just made them work better."

"And how did you do that?" asked Max.

"Wouldn't you like to know? Bet you're trying to make that spare-parts droid of yours work better, aren't you?"

Max snorted.

"We don't need any help. But you do if you don't realize the risk of shutting down the protection."

Max looked directly into Ryan's eyes. For the first time, he wasn't feeling intimidated by Ryan.

"Okay, you can do what you want, but I'm going to have to talk to Dr. Lehrer about it."

"So, basically, you're saying you're a snitch," said Ryan. His teammates chuckled.

"If I have to be a snitch to keep you from being an idiot, then whose fault is that?" said Max.

Ryan's face flushed red. "Okay, Maxie. We were only playing with Joey. The routines are going to be there."

"Like they were written?" asked Max.

Ryan hesitated. "Yeah, like they were written."

Max stared directly at Ryan and refused to look away. He wanted Ryan to understand his resolve. Finally, Max said, "Okay," and walked out. As he passed through the door, he heard laughter behind him. He guessed that Ryan had made a crack at his expense, but Max didn't care.

"Max, what were you doing over there?" asked Hannah.

He answered her with a look that let her know he wanted to be left alone.

"Joey," said Max. "You need to go back to your team."

Without a word, Joey left.

In his dorm room, Max was logged into Roblox. The Skype ringtone came through his headset. He was in the middle of an intense raid and decided not to answer it. Then he thought it might be his dad and clicked the icon. It wasn't his dad; it was Sergey.

Max hesitated a moment and then answered the call.

"Hi, Max," said Sergey. "I saw that you made it into Steve's office. What did you find?"

"I found a folder for Gemini in a filing cabinet," said Max.

"And?"

"All of the files had been deleted. There was nothing there."

"Nothing at all?"

Max shook his head at the camera.

"Who deleted them?" asked Sergey.

"Steve."

"When?"

"About twelve years ago."

Sergey nodded.

"Why would he have done that?" asked Max.

"Steve wanted to push Verner Hoff aside so that he could become CEO. He was trying to convince the board that Verner was crazy and reckless with money. Steve said that if Verner remained in charge of the park, and Hoff Enterprises, the company would go bankrupt. He used Project Gemini as the example. He said that it was a crazy idea and Verner's insistence on pushing it proved he was unfit to remain in charge. The board agreed and ordered Project Gemini shut down. Verner went along, but kept it going under the radar. When Steve found out the project was being secretly funded he went ballistic and the project was finally shut down. The shock must have been what killed Verner."

Max paused for a moment to take in this new information.

"But why would Steve want to delete all of the Gemini files?"

"Because he didn't understand it and was afraid the information might come back to haunt him. He wanted to get rid of any evidence. He does that a lot."

"So why does he want it now?" asked Max.

Sergey shrugged. "That's a good question. I think it's because he finally realized what Gemini was and what it would mean for the company and the world. Steve needs a new breakthrough for himself and Hoff Industries, and he thinks Project Gemini is it."

Max heard a beep in his headset. One of his Roblox buddies was pinging him. "Sergey, I have to go. What do we do now?"

"We keep looking for that chip. It's out there. We just have to find it."

Max closed the Skype window and sighed. He didn't want to have to sneak back into Steve's office to use the helmet. Max noticed the thumb drive lying beside the computer.

Max messaged his friend: I'll be there in a few minutes.

He slid the drive into the USB port on the right side of his laptop. The computer beeped as it recognized the drive. Max accessed the drive's main directory and started looking around. In less than ten seconds he found what he suspected was there. Max double-clicked on the icon, hoping he hadn't launched a virus that would destroy his computer.

A login window appeared. Max's fingers seemed to have a mind of their own as they typed in a username and password. The laptop display flashed and Max was in.

Max didn't know how long he had been in the virtual library when he heard a soft knock at his door. "Yeah?" he said.

Hannah poked her head in. "Whatcha' doin?"

"Come here," said Max.

"Look at this! This is what I saw in the helmet. This drive." Max pointed to the thumb drive.

"It works with regular computers, too. The helmet is just an interface. The emulator is what does the work."

Hannah looked at the screen. "What is this?"

Max's eyes were wide, his pupils dilated. His head bobbed with excess energy. "It's everything! I get it now. It's just ones and zeros. All of the computers and equipment and rides; everything in the park that's electronic made real. You can see it."

"Looks like a game to me," said Hannah.

At first Max was annoyed. Then he started bobbing his head. "It is, kind of. But I've thought for a long time that there's something real about games. They're like being in a different place. This is the same, but it's part of the physical world, too."

"You mean like another dimension?"

"It is, isn't it? This whole other world that's around us, but we can't see. This," Max said pointed to the thumb drive, "is our way in."

"So, what are you going to do with it?" asked Hannah.

"Find Gemini. This will lead us to Project Gemini."

CHAPTER 18

Max was running to catch up with his teammates after staying behind to make sure that Dexter's data was backing up properly. It was early evening, Max's favorite time of day in the park. After sunset, the crowds thinned out, the temperature dropped, and lights along the walkways blinked on. The dome overhead was lit with small lights like LED stars.

One benefit of his special status was that Max could go places the other scholars couldn't. Access to the maintenance passageways greatly reduced the time it took to get around. Max was cutting behind the Constellation Theater on his way to the Quasar when the back door of the theater opened, and a girl stepped out.

"Excuse me," said Max as he dodged her and continued on his way.

"Max." the girl said.

He turned and had to look at her for a second before he realized it was Kaylee. She looked so normal in regular clothes and without makeup.

"Oh, hi, Kaylee. How's it going?" Max was so surprised that he didn't have time to be embarrassed or nervous.

"I'm fine. Time to go home," said Kaylee with a shrug.

"Where's your mom?" Max asked.

"She's already left. A driver's taking me home." Kaylee paused and looked down. "Max, about the ball the other night."

Max avoided looking at Kaylee and said, "It's okay."

"No, it's not. I could see it in your eyes. You were disappointed in me."

Max looked up at the dome, struggling for something to say. "Why would you put up with that? You could have gone to the Ball with anyone."

Max saw Kaylee blush. "It's not like that Max. I don't know anyone except for people in the business, and people like that aren't your friends."

"Yeah, but Ryan?"

"I know Max. But he's more like me."

"What do you mean?"

"Shallow."

Max shook his head. "You're not shallow. You're a performer, but you're not shallow."

"How do you know?"

"Because you wouldn't be here talking to me if you were shallow. You wouldn't care what I think about you."

"That's sweet, Max. I know I'm not smart like you guys, but I like talking to you."

"You're as smart as anyone, just in a different way. And much more talented."

Kaylee smiled and hugged him. At first, Max let his arms hang limp, then he hugged back.

Kaylee pulled away. "Friends?"

"Definitely."

"I have to go, the driver's waiting," said Kaylee as she turned and walked away.

Ding-dong. Bzzzzzz.

Sergey rose from his chair and moved quickly down the hall. The buzzing of the stuck doorbell was extremely annoying.

Sergey opened the door, ignored the man standing on the porch, and started jiggling the plastic doorbell button. "I hate this thing," he said, more to himself than the man standing there.

"Let me see," said Dieter Lehrer. "I used to have one like this." Dieter flicked the button with his middle finger, and the buzzing stopped. "You really should replace that."

Sergey grunted. "I don't have time for that sort of crap." For the first time since opening the door, Sergey looked at his guest. "Pardon me. Please come in. I'm not used to visitors."

As Sergey stepped aside to let Dieter enter, he looked around his living room and saw that his house wasn't prepared to receive visitors either. Every piece of furniture was covered with something. Two armchairs were piled with clothes, and on the single table were two open boxes. Packing peanuts lay scattered across the table and floor.

"Let's go to the kitchen," said Sergey, leading the way.

The kitchen was in worse condition, but at least there were two empty chairs where they could sit once Sergey cleared away the pizza boxes and Chinese food containers.

"Would you like a piece of pizza?" Sergey asked Dieter. "It's just from last night. I can nuke it, and it's as good as fresh."

Dieter shook his head and grimaced. "No thank you, I just ate."

Sergey motioned for Dieter to sit down. He took the other chair. "It has been a while, Dieter. How are things at the park? What's new?"

Those weren't the questions Sergey wanted to ask. In fact, he didn't want to ask any questions at all. For years, he and Dieter had been meeting from time to time to share Scientopia-related news. Sergey was eager to make a deposit into the gossip bank, for a change.

"Oh, you know how it is," said Dieter. "Things are much the same. We're well into the Summer Genius program. A very promising group of young people this year. They may help us make some progress in understanding Alistair. Steve's still bumbling about as usual. In fact, he wanted me to get rid of one of our best students, Max Powers. The child has exceptional insight and an unusual connection to the park. Extraordinary really."

Sergey could restrain himself no longer. "Yes, Max is quite the find, isn't he?"

Dieter furrowed his brow and looked closely at Sergey. "You know the boy?"

Sergey leaned back in his chair and smiled. "You could say that. We have a sort of connection."

"What do you mean?" asked Dieter.

"I've been working with Max to find Gemini."

Dieter raised his eyebrows.

"And that's not all," said Sergey on the verge of bubbling over. "Do you know who he is?"

Dieter raised his arms and opened his hands in question. "He's just a boy. His father's name is Tim Powers. A very nice man. I met him at the Founder's Ball."

Sergey was slowly shaking his head.

"What do you mean?" asked Dieter.

"Max Powers..." said Sergey, pausing for effect, "...is Verner Hoff's son."

"Nonsense."

"It's true."

"How do you know this?"

Sergey smiled, enjoying his triumph. "Steve found out. The DNA is a match. There's no question."

"And how do you know?"

"I know every keystroke Steve makes. He's very careless, a technical idiot."

Dieter nodded. "Yes, I know what you mean. He's made some shocking statements to me. How does a man like that get into such a position?" Dieter dwelled on the thought for a second before turning back to Sergey. "Does Steve know you know?"

"No, but that's not all. He doesn't want anyone else to know either. He deleted the files."

"But you still have them?" asked Dieter.

"Of course."

"What are you going to do?"

Sergey tossed him a folder stuffed with papers.

"What's this?" asked Dieter suspiciously.

"When I worked at Hoff Enterprises, I never paid much attention to the business side. You and I were doing the real work, and the rest was left to lawyers and accountants." Sergey flushed with anger as he remembered his arrogance and how it had cost him everything.

"I swore I'd never make that mistake again. After my ouster, I made a point of studying everything possible about how Hoff Enterprises was run." Sergey sneered in contempt. "I now know more about the company and its legal structure than their own lawyers."

Dieter opened the folder and looked at the printouts.

"Look at the section titled *Ownership*."

In the event of Verner Hoff's death, his shares shall pass to his legal or natural children. If the children are minors their shares shall be voted in trust by a trustee appointed by the board of directors. If Verner Hoff dies without issue, his shares shall be placed in a trust controlled by the CEO.

Dieter read the section again and slowly closed the folder. "This means our sweet little Max Powers is in line to become an immensely wealthy and powerful person," he said calmly.

"I think that's what we need to talk about. It changes everything, doesn't it? Did you know that when Max turns eighteen he will control enough stock to run the company?"

"It won't do him much good if Steve destroys everything first, will it?" asked Deiter.

"That's right," said Sergey. "But we can fix it."

"How?"

"Project Gemini."

"That old project?"

"Don't you see? The answer has always been Project Gemini. Verner was so close. It would have been the breakthrough of the century then and maybe more so now. Everyone and everything are much more dependent on computers these days. Viable artificial intelligence based on an optical chip would usher in a golden age of technology."

"What makes you think it still exists? You've been looking for it for more than a decade with no luck."

"That was before, Max. I've made more progress in the last few weeks than all those years combined. I don't think he realizes what he's doing."

"So, you get the chip, then what?"

"If I come to them with the chip, the board of directors will have no choice but to put me in charge. To give me back what was wrongfully taken."

Dieter laughed out loud.

"You? Are you serious? You think they're going to put a computer hermit living in filth in charge of a multibillion-dollar company? There's no way the government would allow you near our defense contracts." Dieter laughed again. "I've never heard anything so absurd."

"You think I can't do it? I'm a founder of the company!"

"Yes, but your role was minor. Verner was always the brains behind it all. You have some technical abilities, but like any Russian, no gift for organization. Too emotional. The idea is laughable."

Sergey trembled with rage. "Get out! Get out, you Nazi creep!"

Dieter walked calmly to his car as Sergey slammed the door behind him. Dieter grinned as he walked away from the house, the sound of Sergey screaming and breaking things fading into the distance.

CHAPTER 19

In Team Ritchie's lab, Alistair and Dexter were lying on tables with their chest panels off, exposing their core components. Max stood between the tables, looking first at one ani-droid and then the other. Finally, Max felt like his team was starting to work together. Aiden had started pushing for adding a jetpack again, but Dr. Lehrer let him know in no uncertain terms that jetpacks would never be allowed. Every time Aiden suggested new crazy ideas, Max told him to ask Dr. Lehrer first, and Aiden immediately dropped it.

While the students worked, Alistair maintained a constant chatter; "When are we going to be through, Max? I have a reception in the atrium at 12:00 o'clock. You have to put me back together by then. Are you going to be able to do that?"

"Hey, Aiden," said Max. "What do you think that is under there?"

Aiden shined his flashlight to where Max was pointing. "I can't see anything. That processor is in the way."

Max examined the board the processor was attached to. "I think we can unscrew the board to get a better view."

Alistair raised his head. "Oh no, Max! Don't do that. If you disconnect my primary processor, I'll go dead."

Max looked again into Alistair's open chest. "It won't be a problem, Alistair. I'll leave the wires attached. You'll be fine."

"I don't like this, Max. I'll never make it to the reception. I wish I had a Hoffpop."

"What good would that do you?" said Max as he carefully loosened the first screw. "You can't eat."

"It might make me feel better. It works for everyone else."

Max glanced at Alistair's face, wondering what it would mean for a robot to feel better. "Here you go, Aiden, what do you see in there?"

"A hexagonal crystal," said Aiden.

"What do you think it is?" asked Max.

"Can't tell."

"Let me see." Max carefully shifted the board to give himself a better look. "Hand me the light."

Max took the flashlight from Aiden and moved it around the crystal. "It has writing on it. It says *Alpha*."

"That's all? What do you think it means?"

"I'm not sure, I need to check on something," said Max. Max turned around to peer inside Dexter. After some careful work with his flashlight, he was able to confirm that Dexter didn't have the same sort of crystal chip. The mounts were there, but they were empty.

There was one other thing Max needed to confirm. He went to his computer, took the emulator flash drive from his pocket and slipped it into an empty USB port. On the screen, he navigated to the lab where they were working now. He could see the computers and other equipment in the room, but there was no sign of Alistair.

"I'll be right back," said Max running out of the lab.

"Don't forget me, Max." Alistair moaned.

Max found Greg in the break room. "Greg, I need to use the helmet, can you get it for me?"

"I don't know, Max. I think it's still in Steve's office. What do you need it for?"

Max could sense Greg's reluctance. "We're working on Alistair. I think it would help me get a better view."

"Is that all? You're not going to use it for anything else?"

"No, I promise."

Greg looked into Max's eyes. Max wanted to look away but decided it best not to.

"Okay, Max, I'll have Steve's assistant send it down."

It wasn't long before the helmet arrived and Max had it connected. Before he slipped it on, he noticed Ryan looking at him suspiciously.

With the helmet on, Max was able to navigate quickly to the lab. He saw the partially disassembled Alistair on the table. Max tried to work his way into Alistair's systems. At first he wasn't able to get in. He would move towards Alistair and then bounce off as if hitting an invisible wall. Max approached from several different directions looking for a gap, but he couldn't find one.

Max noticed that his hands were curled into fists. *I need to relax.* Max made himself think of air, an empty space bounded by gray. He slowly started to relax, and his arms dropped to his sides. Max willed himself forward inside Alistair's body. He glided toward the ani-droid and suddenly he had access to Alistair's systems.

It took Max a moment to orient himself. He made his way to the central processor, which he could sense was dormant. As Max moved around the board he began to notice a faint greenish glow. The light was similar to what Max imagined the aurora borealis would be. Periodically he could see sparks, like pinpoint lightning, flash through the green halo.

"Alistair, can you hear me?" Max thought.

"Yes, Max."

Max tried to think of a question that would activate Alistair's AI module. *"Alistair, if you can't make it to the reception, what are you going to do?"*

Instantly there were more lightning flashes than Max could count.

"I would call Ms. Barrett and tell her that I wasn't going to be able to make it. But please, Max, don't make me miss the reception. I'm programmed to be on time, and it would throw off my whole day to miss anything."

"Would that make you feel bad, Alistair?"

Keith Philips

In response, the chip lit up with a variety of colors. For brief instants, the light show appeared white but it always transitioned back into various rainbow hues.

"I would feel bad," said Alistair. "I wouldn't be able to carry enough Hoffpops to make everyone feel better."

Max had seen enough. He had found Project Gemini.

"Come in," said Max.

Hannah pushed open the spring-loaded door with her back, her arms full with her laptop and a box of snacks.

"What did you bring?" said Max as he took the box from under her arm and rifled through it.

"Hello. Nice to see you too, Max. I'm fine, thank you."

Max's mouth was already full of potato chips. "I just saw you at dinner."

"And don't talk with your mouth full, please." Hannah paused with an exasperated expression. "Did you hear that? I already sound like my mother."

Max was looking through the box for his next snack. He held up a bag of baby carrots with a questioning smirk.

"My mom brought them. Go ahead."

"You can keep those."

Hannah shrugged, took the bag from Max, grabbed a carrot, and bit into it with a satisfying *crunch*. "What are we doing?" she asked.

"Now look who's talking with their mouth full."

"Now look who's sounding like my mother," said Hannah, tossing her head from side to side.

"I know what we're looking for now."

Hannah raised her eyebrows.

"The chip. I saw the prototype in Alistair."

"I thought you said it was just another chip," said Hannah.

"I didn't want anyone to know."

144

"Max, they already know that Alistair has an optical chip in him."

"It's not just that!" Max lowered his voice. "It was glowing green when he was functioning normally, but when I asked him how something made him feel, it lit up in different colors. Do you know what that means?"

Hannah nodded yes, then stopped. "Actually, no, I don't."

"That was Alistair's artificial intelligence programming at work."

"You could see the program running?"

"Not exactly," said Max. "But I could tell that's what was going on. Don't you see? Alistair's AI program is in the chip! It's part of the chip. That's why no one can find it."

Hannah's eyes grew wide. "You mean, all of the logic and routines are built into the chip? There's no compiling! That would make it run that much faster."

"And the different colors. Do you realize what that means?"

Hannah pushed a few curls off her forehead and thought. "There are different spectrums of light. Max! The chip can handle multiple wavelengths of light going through the same pathways! It's like a different processor for each color."

Max beamed. The thing he liked best about Hannah was her ability to grasp cool and nerdy ideas. "The optical chip is already super-fast, but now it's like a million core processor!"

"But if the AI code is integrated into the chip," mused Hannah, "then why don't you just tell Steve? Why do you want to keep it a secret?"

"If Steve found out, he'd take Alistair apart. He hasn't tried to reverse-engineer the optical chip, but if he knows the AI programming is hidden inside, then he wouldn't hesitate to pull the chip from Alistair."

"Alistair would still function, wouldn't he?"

"It would be like a lobotomy to him. His 'brain' would be gone. He would be like every other ani-droid."

"I guess we better start looking for this other chip, right?" asked Hannah.

"We now have a general idea of what it looks like, and it glows green in the emulator. It wouldn't be doing any AI work. All we have to do is search the park. It has to be here."

"It's a big park."

"Well, it won't be just anywhere," said Max. "It's probably in the Crystal Tower. Start up your computer. I've made a copy of the thumb drive for you. With two of us, it will go twice as fast."

Max moved Hannah to the side of the double desk opposite him. Earlier he had been disappointed that he hadn't been assigned a roommate, but there were advantages. Max plugged the emulator into Hannah's computer and showed her how to use it. "Let's start with Steve's office. I'll be there in a minute."

Max went to his computer and logged on.

"Where do I start?" asked Hannah.

"You take the right side, and I'll take the left."

It was fun poking around in Steve's office without the risk of getting caught. Every few minutes Max or Hannah would call the other over to take a look at something interesting. After a while, there were fewer new things to look at, and they began to make more progress. Still, it was after 11:00 PM before they finished Steve's office.

"Next floor?" asked Max.

"Sure."

The next time Max looked at the clock, it read 2:07 AM. He had fallen asleep. Hannah had, too.

"Hannah, wake up. If they catch you in here, we're going to be in trouble."

"Okay," said Hannah as she lifted her head. She slowly got up and left without bothering to take her computer. Max turned out the light and crawled in bed.

Morning came too soon, and Max could barely open his eyes when he heard the alarm. He had to cross the room to turn it off. *A couple more minutes won't hurt* he thought to himself as he lay back down.

A pounding at the door, "Max, wake up! You're late." It was Jimmy.

"I'm coming."

Max pulled on his clothes, regretting that he didn't have time to take a shower. Hot water would have helped him wake up, but it was too late now.

As he entered the lab, Max saw that Hannah was in no better shape.

"Good morning, Max," she said without enthusiasm.

Max nodded. He didn't feel like talking. He was so sleepy that it startled him when Greg started talking. Max hadn't seen him come in.

"Good morning, Team Ritchie. How's it going? Feel like you're ready for the big competition on Thursday?" Greg said in an annoyingly cheerful voice.

There was a muffled cough, but no one said anything.

"I'm sure you all will do fine. The main event today is the practice with Kaylee. Each team will have an hour with her to work out any bugs in the routine. We're going in reverse order today so you'll need to have Dexter over to the Constellation Theater and ready to go in thirty minutes."

The prospect of seeing Kaylee helped pull Max closer to full consciousness, but he was still dragging on the way to the Constellation Theater. He was happy that Aiden and Jimmy were alert, so he could follow them without having to think.

In the theater, Aiden took charge of positioning Dexter on stage. Alistair was already there. Max gave him a feeble, "Hi," and slumped to the stage floor as the others fussed over Dexter, and led him through his steps. Max watched silently. After a few minutes, his head started to buzz. *I should have gotten more sleep,* he thought. He was sitting on the floor cross-legged with his elbows on his knees and his chin in his hands when Kaylee came on stage.

Max stood up immediately and smiled, his exhaustion forgotten. He locked eyes with Kaylee, and she walked directly to him, beaming. When she got to him, she reached out and touched his arm. "Hey, Max. I'm so glad to see you. This is going to be so much fun."

Max grinned and looked around at his classmates, who seemed to be looking at him funny. Their confusion barely registered with Max. His head was light with a new burst of energy.

Practice began. The choreographer was standing by, but she didn't have much to do. Kaylee was familiar with the routine and took charge with ease.

The plan for the competition was that every droid would perform a duet with Kaylee. The choreographer assured the kids that each team's routine was equally difficult.

Kaylee went through the steps slowly with Dexter. Everything was going well until a change step at the end of the song proved too complicated for Dexter. Each time he tried it he came dangerously close to losing his balance.

"What do you think is wrong?" Jimmy asked Max.

"Maybe it's too hard for him," offered Hannah. "Let's see if Alistair can do it."

Kaylee showed Alistair the move, which he repeated easily.

"Should I try it again with Dexter?" Kaylee asked Max.

Max looked up from his computer. "No, Dexter will do the same thing every time."

"Why?" asked Kaylee. "Alistair was able to get it."

"That's because Alistair can learn. Dexter can't, he doesn't have the chip or AI module in him. The only things he can do is what we program in." Max shifted his attention back to the screen and kept talking. "It doesn't matter. I think I've found the problem. We messed up the instructions."

A minute later Max looked up from his computer. "Okay, I've sent the new instructions to Dexter, try it now."

Kaylee started the steps again from the beginning. This time, Dexter made it through without any errors.

"Good!" said Kaylee. "That was better. We'll go through the steps one more time and then do it with music."

"You can do it with music now," said Max. "Once we have the steps programmed right he'll go through it the same way every time. He can't do anything different. Just make sure you don't change anything. He can't improvise."

"All right then, with music," said Kaylee. The music started, and Dexter went straight through the routine. Once the singing was added Max had to make a few adjustments, but from then it was perfect, with time to spare.

The choreographer spoke up. "All right people, we're done. Kaylee, you can take fifteen until the next team. Thank you, everyone."

Kaylee walked to the back of the stage. She picked up a towel and wiped her forehead as she watched Team Ritchie getting ready to leave. Max looked back at her and waved goodbye. Kaylee motioned for him to come over.

"Max, that was awesome. How did you learn so much about computers?" Kaylee asked.

Max shrugged slightly. "Just something I like," he said. Max felt his heart flutter.

"You're very talented," Kaylee said as she gave him a hug.

Kaylee pulled back but left her hands on Max's shoulders. His hands were on her waist. There was a pause. Max didn't know what to do, so he leaned forward and prepared to kiss her.

Kaylee pulled back, her hands blocking Max's lips. "Max," she said. "It's not like that. We're just friends."

Max blushed. "I know. I just didn't know what I was doing."

"All right," said Kaylee. "I'll forgive you. This time."

Max forced a laugh and turned to leave. That's when he saw Hannah standing at the front of the stage, staring at him. She did *not* look happy.

Hannah turned and ran from the stage. Max stood and watched, debating what he should do. He ran after her.

Outside the theater, Max didn't see Hannah anywhere. He assumed she would head back to her room, and he started off in that direction. He rounded a corner and caught a glimpse of her running through the thin morning crowd. Just as Max picked up his pace to intercept Hannah he heard someone shout, "Max!"

Max stopped and looked around for the source of the voice. It took him a second but then he noticed a park custodian, dressed in silver overalls with a handlebar mustache and beard. It was Sergey.

"Max, it's me, Sergey."

"Really?" Max said, not trying to hide the sarcasm.

"Yeah, good disguise, isn't it? I noticed so many of the younger men are wearing facial hair now. I blend right in."

"Yeah, I saw one of those in a Throwback Thursday Bullwinkle cartoon."

"Honestly?" said Sergey as he stroked his mustache. "I noticed you've been using the emulator. Have you found anything?"

"Not yet."

"You'll tell me when you do?"

"Yeah. Hey, I've got to go. There's somewhere I need to be." Max turned to run then stopped.

"Sergey, what is it you want to do with the chip anyway?"

Sergey started to speak, then stopped. He nervously touched his mustache. "This chip is not for me, Max. It's too powerful for one person or even one company. It should be free for everyone to use."

Max didn't know what to think, but he did know that he didn't trust Sergey. His answer sounded too much like what he might think Max would want to hear.

"Okay."

"Max, I think it's time to tell you more about your mother."

Max froze. "What?"

"She was on a private, chartered flight when she died."

Max squinted at Sergey. "So?"

"Everyone on board was involved with Project Gemini. Someone paid to reassemble the team so they could finish the job. Someone with very deep pockets. You find the chip, and next time we meet I'll give you more details. Agreed?"

Max wasn't sure what to say. He'd been told his mother was on a flight to a job interview when the plane crashed, but he had no idea the job was related to Project

Gemini. "But I thought Steve terminated Project Gemini years before that."

"He did. But five years later, he, or someone else, wanted to finish it." Sergey stared hard at Max. "Your mother gave her life for this project. Can I count on you?

"Yes. I have to go now." Max turned and ran after Hannah.

CHAPTER 20

Max was all nerves as he sat next to Hannah in the Constellation Theater, waiting for the final ani-droid competition to begin. The theater was packed. Of course, all of the Summer Genius scholars, plus many of their family members, were there. It seemed as if all of the Scientopia engineering staff were present. Max's head was starting to buzz again, making it difficult to concentrate.

Three ani-droids sat in chairs at the back of the stage, each waiting for its turn to perform. Max noticed that the hooded cloak Hannah had put over Dexter had shifted slightly revealing his black jeans, sneakers and white socks. Steve stood on the edge of the stage, shuffling papers. He would deliver opening remarks. After that, Alistair would take over as emcee. Max had an uneasy feeling. He looked up and saw that Steve was staring at him. When Steve saw that Max had noticed him, he looked away.

"Isn't this exciting?" asked Hannah.

He turned and saw that she was talking to Joey, sitting next to her on the other side. Things had been chilly between Max and Hannah since the incident with Kaylee. It wasn't like Hannah was his girlfriend, but Max had apologized anyway. He wasn't exactly sure what he had apologized for, but he didn't see another way out. Hannah had said everything was okay, but it was clear she thought his apology hadn't been entirely sincere.

Steve tapped the microphone, which buzzed loudly. The audience groaned in protest. "Ha ha. Sorry. Let's try that again. Welcome, Scientopia friends and family to the final Summer Genius robotics competition."

Steve paused and waited for the applause to subside. "Our Summer Geniuses have never been given a more difficult challenge, and they have risen to the occasion. In a few moments, you're going to see an exceptional display of robotic dexterity, all of which has been engineered by our young associates. Regardless of the outcome, every team member has a right to be proud of their accomplishments. Now, I'm going to turn the program over to everyone's favorite ani-droid, Scientopia's own Alistair."

The audience clapped loudly as Alistair took his place at the podium.

"Thank you, thank you," said Alistair. "You're much too kind. Please."

As the applause faded, Alistair resumed. "Welcome everyone. Behind me, you see the, um, three..." Alistair coughed, and the scholars started laughing. Alistair laughed himself. "I'm sorry everyone, perhaps I should explain. We had a little mishap yesterday with the Team Shannon entry, and he won't be able to compete today."

"What happened?" someone shouted from the back.

Alistair's eyes opened wide and swept the audience, causing more laughter. "Why don't we just say the Team Shannon entry had as many lives as a duck and took to water like a cat."

The scholars roared, remembering the mechanical mess that had been fished from the water after a guest asked to be taken to the lake.

"We'll go ahead and get started then. We have drawn straws, and first up is Team McCarthy." Alistair turned to the ani-droids, sitting motionless in their chairs at the back of the stage. "Buck, are you ready?"

Buck, the Team McCarthy ani-droid, stood and trundled forward toward the audience. His team thought it would be cool to make him walk as if he were on the surface of the moon. The ani-droid's altered gait made him bob from side to side as he came forward. That, combined with the overstuffed white astronaut gear he was wearing, made Buck look like he had soiled his suit.

Giggles from those who noticed rippled through the auditorium.

The music started with a muted trumpet. Kaylee sang the first line: "Stars shining bright above you."

Everyone laughed. *Someone has a sense of humor,* thought Max. Buck completed his routine competently. He was good enough that if the other ani-droids blew it, Team McCarthy was certainly still in the competition.

The next ani-droid up was Rob of Team Turing. When Alistair called him, the tall black ani-droid stood and took a bow. The audience clapped, and he waved. The move wasn't a part of the required script, and Max thought it was a nice touch. Kaylee and Rob took their places, waiting for the music to start.

Max heard Joey whisper to Hannah "We've got this. Can't lose." Max felt a shiver of alarm. He suddenly felt stupid for not making sure that Ryan had kept the protection program in place.

Max leaned forward and whispered, "What did you do? Did Ryan disable the protection?"

Joey looked startled that anyone but Hannah had heard.

The music started. The tune was *Don't Go Breaking My Heart.*

"No," whispered Joey over the music, "we just made him want to win."

Max sat back in his seat and looked at the stage, but none of the activity there registered. He was trying to figure out how you make an ani-droid *want to win.*

The audience had started swaying to the music, and Max pushed the swirl of thoughts from his mind to watch Rob. The robot was surprisingly good for such a big, ominous-looking machine. Team Turing had programmed a lot of subtlety into his performance; with well-timed glances, head bobs, and body swaying. Even though Rob's face was covered with a helmet-like mask,

Keith Philips

eliminating any possibility of facial expressions, he gave the impression he was enjoying himself.

When the song was over the applause lasted for several minutes. Team Turing started cheering, which spread to the audience. Kaylee and Rob were standing on stage hand in hand. Kaylee looked at Rob and said something. He nodded and they both took a bow. The cheering grew louder.

Joey leaned around Hannah. "See!"

Max had to admit; it was an exceptional performance, possibly a winning one.

Alistair started speaking.

"Wasn't that something? I think those two may have some things to talk about after the show if you know what I mean," he said with an exaggerated wink. The audience laughed again.

"Now it's time for our final performance, and then we'll turn it over to the judges to decide on the winning team for this year's Summer Genius competition. Put your hands together for Dexter!"

Dexter stood and dropped his cloak to the floor. Underneath the cloak, his pudgy shell was stuffed into black jeans and a white tee shirt. Over the shirt was a white letterman's sweater with the red letters "SG" on the front. A black wig covered his bald head. Dexter was every bit the '50s greaser. The audience, especially the parents, started clapping. Dexter strode to the front of the stage like he owned it. Even the scholars from the other teams laughed. It was too much; nothing like the funny, mild-mannered Dexter they were used to. Kaylee joined in the fun and raised her eyebrows with a "Who's this guy?" expression.

By the time the first bars of *You're the One that I Want*, started to pulse through the theater, the audience knew what was coming, and they roared their approval.

Max smiled. If audience response had anything to do with the judging, it looked like they still had a chance. As Max watched Dexter take off his letterman's sweater, swing it overhead, and throw it into the audience, he happened to notice Rob. It struck him as odd that the ani-droid was alert. Max looked at Buck for a comparison. Buck was still.

Max looked back at Rob. The big black ani-droid would look at Kaylee and Dexter for a moment, then turn his head to the audience and back. The longer Max watched, the more rapid Rob's movements became. By the time Kaylee was singing, "To my heart, I must be true..." Max saw that Rob's right arm was twitching.

Something was wrong with Rob. The ani-droid needed to be shut down. Max's mind raced for a way to do it. It was hard to think with Kaylee and Dexter singing and the buzzing in his head getting louder. There was nothing he could do.

Max stood up.

"What are you doing?" asked Hannah. She tried to pull him back into his seat. Max pulled free of her grasp. He looked for the quickest way to the aisle and realized it would take forever to squeeze past everyone in their seats. Without thinking, Max stood on his seat and stepped over the back of the row in front of him. His foot hit the armrest between two people and slid off, causing him to crash down onto other kids.

"Hey! What the..." he heard someone shouting in protest.

Max tumbled forward into the empty space in front of the stage. A murmur of voices rose up from the crowd as people tried to figure out what was happening.

The music continued to play.

Max stood up and looked up at Rob. The ani-droid was now trembling uncontrollably. Max ran to the closest steps onto the stage and took them two at a time. Max had no idea what he was going to do. There was only one thought in his head: *Rob had to be stopped.* There was no telling what the powerful ani-droid might do.

"Rob, stop!" Max shouted. He didn't know if Rob or anyone else had heard him over the music. Max kept running up the stairs. "Rob, terminate! Rob, shutdown!" Max was screaming as he ran, saying anything he could think of that might get through to the ani-droid.

Kaylee saw Max coming up the stairs and stopped singing. Dexter continued with his performance, the music blaring in the background. By the time Max reached the top of the stairs, he realized Rob was focused on Kaylee and Dexter.

Max bolted towards Rob. He was amazed at how slowly everything seemed to move. How he was aware of everything going on in the theater, from the people in the audience who were starting to rise, to the music, to Alistair standing motionless at the side of the stage. Then there was Kaylee. She looked directly at Max in uncomprehending confusion, her back to Rob.

Max had to focus on Rob. The ani-droid was standing fully upright now and moving forward with menacing strides. There wasn't much time.

Max had a clear path to Rob, but no plan for how to stop him. Reaching Rob was one thing, stopping him would be another. Max frantically tried to come up with a plan.

Again Max screamed, "Stop, Rob!"

Another step, and the music stopped. Max sensed Alistair had turned it off. He thought once again about how slowly everything was moving, and about the sheer number of thoughts flowing through his mind, each recognized and considered.

It was at that instant that Max started his swerve away from Rob. His mind, as fast as it was working, still had offered no plan for dealing with the animated machine.

Max had realized his chances of stopping the big ani-droid were slim; that no matter what small thing he would be able to do, Rob's rage would continue. Max could tell that all of Rob's dangerous attention was focused in one place, on Kaylee. The best, the only, thing to do was to move her out of harm's way. It was simple really; take care of Kaylee first, and then Rob. Two steps more.

With each of those two steps Kaylee's eyes grew wider. The threat of Rob from behind had still not registered with her. Her growing alarm was focused only on her friend, Max, and his strange charge across the stage.

By the time Max crashed into Kaylee his focus had already shifted to Rob. Kaylee tumbled to the floor, out of Rob's path. Max was right at Rob. One particular part of the big ani-droid caught his attention. In the gap between Rob's chest plate and hip assembly Max saw a cable. It was the leg harness. Wrapped in it were the power and control wires that ran Rob's legs. Max knew that the cable was attached to a plug. A good yank would pull it out, causing Rob to crumple to the ground, unable to move.

Max had his plan. He was stumbling, off balance from the crash into Kaylee. Falling forward. A step away. He pushed off from the ground in a wild lunge. Max extended his hand in front of him, fingers open, ready to grasp the cable.

It was too much, the lunge. Rob still moved forward. They were too close, moving together too fast. Max crumpled up against Rob like Play Doh thrown against a brick wall. The ani-droid was solid, shockingly immovable. Max felt himself being lifted into the air. He was in Rob's arms. Far in the background was a wail of screaming. Then the sensation of flying, then falling. A dull thump.

Rob had thrown Max halfway across the stage. He had landed on his back with the thud of a dropped bag of sand. Max was struggling for air. He felt like he was drowning. Max was dimly aware that the landing had knocked the breath out of him. His struggle for air and the bright light overhead were the only things he was conscious of.

The light dimmed, and Max squinted to see what was happening. A black silhouette was blocking the light. It was Rob, leaning over, raising his arms over his head. Rob was unstoppable. There were no limits, no control. Max was about to die, crushed by a rampaging ani-droid. Max closed his eyes and hoped it would be quick.

"I'll stop him, Max."

Max realized the voice was in his head. It was Alistair.

Max opened his eyes but the only thing he could see was Rob, his arms raised to crush him. As the arms started down Max sensed movement in the corner of his eye. There was a blur in front of him and a sharp crack of plastic meeting plastic. There followed a thud, and a terrific din of machines crashing to the floor and flailing as they slid across the floor.

"Grab his leg cables!" shouted Max.

Alistair's right hand shot toward Rob's midsection. Almost too quickly to see, Rob clamped his left hand around Alistair's wrist and held it tight. Alistair tried to move, but the raging robot was much stronger. There was a muted crack as the plastic skin of Alistair's arm began to split.

Max raised his head. He saw Alistair, halfway across the stage floor on top of Rob. Rob had Alistair firmly in his grip and was rolling himself to get on top. With Rob's superior strength it was only going to take a few seconds. Then Alistair would be in the same fix Max was three seconds ago. Max tried to get up, but his stomach hurt so much he could barely rise to his hands and knees.

Alistair began shouting, "Max! Get down! Everyone down! Everyone down!"

160

Max knew that Alistair *wouldn't* let Rob hurt anyone and that he was running out of time and options. He knew what his friend had to do. *No!* Max screamed inside his head.

It's the only way. Max heard Alistair reply. Look away, Max. Goodbye.

Alistair was right; this was the only way. Max closed his eyes and covered his head. *Goodbye.*

Max heard a deafening roar as Alistair ignited his hydrogen tanks. He felt the shock wave as it pushed him across the floor. Less than a second later another shock wave hit as Rob's tanks exploded. Max curled into a ball as bits of plastic and metal rained from above. The last thing Max was aware of was screaming and the acrid smell of melted plastic and fried electronics.

CHAPTER 21

When Max regained consciousness, he didn't open his eyes. He could hear people talking quietly and could smell the distinctive odor of a hospital. Max was scared to open his eyes. He was afraid of what they might show him. He performed a mental inventory and realized that he still seemed to have all his limbs and that he wasn't in too much pain. He ached. Everywhere. There was a bandage wrapped around the top of his head and under his chin.

Max tried to replay the last few minutes before he lost consciousness. He remembered the chaos in the theater after the explosion and being wheeled out on a gurney. Hannah and Kaylee were there as he was lifted into the ambulance. *They were safe.* Reassured, and curious, Max opened his eyes.

"Hey, Max."

It was his father. He was in a hospital - the same Scientopia emergency medical clinic he had been taken to after the accident with the helmet. There was a nurse busy adjusting equipment next to his bed.

Max looked at his dad. "Alistair?"

Mr. Powers shook his head. "Gone."

"Anyone else?"

"Everyone is fine, Max."

Max looked at himself. "What about me?"

"You have some burns on your side, arm, and face, but the doctor says they're not serious."

"I'm thirsty," said Max.

The nurse went to the table at the foot of his bed and poured Max a cup of water. He drank it eagerly.

"What now?" asked Max.

"I don't know what will happen, Max. This is a big shock to everyone. I think it will take a while to sort things out."

"I want to see what happened, Dad. I want to go back there. Now."

"Max, you've been injured. You need to stay here until the doctors say it's okay to leave."

"How long with that be?"

"I don't know."

Max knew he couldn't argue his way out. Instead, he put on his sad face. He didn't push it too far. Just enough to get the sympathy he needed.

"I'll ask the doctor," said Mr. Powers.

Mr. Powers stepped into the hall and returned with a middle-aged man in a lab coat. The doctor regarded Max skeptically.

"I don't think you need to be going anywhere young man. You've had too much excitement already."

"Just for a little bit," said Max. "I need to see. It's bothering me."

The emotional appeal worked. "Very well," said the doctor. "I guess it wouldn't hurt for your dad to push you over in a wheelchair. Take a quick look and come right back. Okay, Max?"

"Yes, sir."

Yellow tape surrounded the Constellation Theater, and a security guard stood by the door. A sign said that all performances were cancelled until further notice. Max asked his dad to wheel him to the back door. It might be easier to get in that way.

The back door was propped open with a steady stream of people coming and going. Mr. Powers pushed Max right in, down a short hall, and to the double backstage doors on the left-hand side of the stage.

Curtains blocked Max's view of everything except the right-hand side of the stage. Steve, Greg, Dr. Lehrer, Kaylee, and someone Max didn't know were standing in a group talking. As his dad pushed the wheelchair forward, the center of the stage became visible. There were technicians with brooms sweeping ani-droid fragments into a pile.

Mr. Powers pushed Max a dozen more feet before he was able to see what remained of Alistair and Rob. Untouched since the explosion, locked in a motionless struggle, were the mangled and melted remains of his friend and Ryan's mechanical monster. A short distance away Dexter lay mostly intact, but clearly broken and immobile.

"Max!"

Max knew before looking who it was. He turned his head toward Kaylee. She had broken away from the group and was running towards him.

"Are you okay?" Kaylee said, bending down to him. "You're not hurt, are you?"

Max's father answered. "He has some minor burns, but the doctor says he'll be fine."

Kaylee moved to bring her face level with Max's. "Max, you saved me! I was so scared. How did you know?"

Max lowered his head. "It was nothing."

"It was something to me." Kaylee said while trying to give him a hug.

"Here's our hero," said Steve as the rest of the group approached Max's wheelchair.

"Max, Scientopia owes you a debt of gratitude. There's no telling what would have happened if you hadn't realized that Rob was malfunctioning. I don't know how you knew, but you certainly saved the day."

Max saw the man he didn't know touch Steve's arm. When Steve looked at him, the man shook his head slightly. It seemed like this stranger was giving Steve orders.

"I have to go now," said Steve while placing his hand on Max's shoulder. "Thanks again, Max."

Steve and the unidentified man left through the backstage doors.

"How did you know that Rob was going to attack, Max?" asked Greg.

"Someone told me that Team Turing had modified his code and when I noticed his strange behavior I knew something was wrong."

"Whatever it was," said Dr. Lehrer, "I have never seen anything braver. You attacked that beast with no concern at all for your own safety. What were you hoping to do?"

"I don't know exactly. I was trying to grab his belly cable. I was trying to give everyone time to get away." Max paused. "Instead, Alistair saved us all."

Dr. Lehrer nodded his head sadly and looked towards Alistair's remains. "That's true, Max. We all owe *both* of you a debt of gratitude."

Max glanced again at the scorched and twisted anidroids. "Can I take a closer look?" he asked Dr. Lehrer.

"Sure, Max."

Max started to rise from his chair.

"Max?" said his father.

"I'll be all right, Dad." Max stood. He winced as the bandages rubbed against his burns, but ignored the pain and limped over to the two bodies. The explosion and burning hydrogen had melted their shells into the actuators and other electronics. There was nothing recognizable left of either. Black lumps of plastic from Rob mixed with yellowish plastic from Alistair, wires, and twisted metal.

Max turned his attention to Dexter. He was damaged but still in one piece.

Finally, Max limped over to the pile of debris at center stage. He bent down and ran his hand through the collection of washers, hydraulic pistons, pieces of circuit boards and bits of plastic. All of the things that, when put together, had made something almost human. A glimmer of gold caught Max's attention. He extracted a small round piece of metal from the pile. It was no more than an inch across. It looked like a coin with a broken rivet on each side. Max could see indentations on one side that may have been caused by the explosion. The reverse was engraved with the word **Alistair**.

Max took the gold disc to Dr. Lehrer and asked, "What's this?"

Dr. Lehrer examined the disc. "I don't know, Max. I haven't seen this before. It looks like a nameplate."

"Can I have it?"

Dr. Lehrer turned the disc over again while Max waited for a response.

"I suppose so, Max. You've earned it," he said handing the disc back to Max.

"Is there any way we can rebuild him? Make another one?" asked Max.

Greg replied, "This may be the end of our ani-droid program, Max. At least for a while. Mr. Plant, our government liaison, was saying that the park can't afford the liability of a rampaging robot, and we have other projects that are more important."

"But Alistair never caused any trouble."

"I know, Max. But sometimes when something like this happens the good gets swept out with the bad."

Max nodded. He suddenly felt drained. Mr. Powers helped him back into his wheelchair.

"Can we go back now, Dad?"

CHAPTER 22

"Good morning, Son."

"Good morning, Dad."

Max had spent the night after Alistair's destruction in the Scientopia hospital. His dad stayed with him, sleeping on a chair that folded out into a bed.

"How do you feel?"

"Better."

The pain from Max's burns had been reduced to a dull ache by painkillers. The doctors said he would have to keep the bandages on his side, arm, and face for a couple more days.

"You ready to go home?"

"Dad, I want to stay. It's just a few more days."

"Okay," said his father. "I think you deserve that."

"Dad, I'm sorry."

"What do you have to be sorry for?"

"For everything that happened. It was my fault. I knew something bad was going on."

"What did you know, Max?"

Max told his father about how he had discovered Ryan trying to eliminate the protection module and confronted him.

"And he promised to keep the protection module in place?"

"Yeah."

Mr. Power's put his hand on Max's head. "Max, the only thing you did was trust someone who let you down. That happens to all of us. It's not your fault."

"But if I had gone to Dr. Lehrer none of this would have happened."

"You don't know that. Your life will be full of what-ifs. You won't be able to live it if you're always looking back at them. Besides, Max, you're just a kid. No reasonable person expects anything from a kid except to do your best. Did you do your best with what you knew at the time?"

"I think so."

"Then there's nothing to worry about. Just keep doing your best, Max, and you'll never have anything to worry about."

Max wanted to take an APT to the Crystal Tower by himself, but his dad wanted to go with him to see the lab. They sat in silence on the ride over. Max couldn't stop thinking about what had happened at the theater. He still needed time to process it all. After this, going back to school was going to seem like a vacation.

In the atrium of the Crystal Tower, the Death Star was lit up like a soccer ball. Max remembered that the World Cup started recently, but he had been too busy to pay attention. They took the clear lift up to the lab. The ride still made Max a bit nervous, but not as much as the first time.

After exiting the lift, they took the curved glass-walled hallway around to the entrance at the rear of the classroom. As they entered Max saw that everything seemed like it was back to normal. The Summer Geniuses were standing and lounging on desks, talking and goofing off. Most of the kids were talking with their friends, not necessarily their teammates. Most of the groups were either all girls or all boys. An exception was Hannah and Joey. Hannah was seated at her desk, Joey standing in front of her, talking. Max saw Ryan sitting alone.

"I'll leave my computer here," Max said to his father, "then we'll take a look at the lab. Wait here, I'll be right back." Max moved toward his desk. After a couple of steps the chatter died. Max looked around for whatever had caught everyone's attention.

All eyes were focused on him.

Someone started clapping. That person was soon joined by another, and another, until everyone, even Ryan, was applauding. Max froze. He hadn't expected this and didn't know how to respond. The people closest to him started shouting "Good job!" and "Way to go, Max!"

Hannah came up to him, took him by the arm, and guided him to his desk. Max remembered his father, looked back up to the door and saw him smiling. Mr. Powers shook his head and waved goodbye. The clapping stopped when Max sat down. For a few seconds, it was hard for Max to focus. He knew that Hannah was asking him questions, and he was answering them; but later he couldn't remember what he had said.

A few minutes later everything settled down as Dr. Lehrer came in to start class. "Scholars," he said. "We have a lot to talk about. Yesterday was a very unfortunate day. Without the brave actions of your classmate, and Alistair's sacrifice, it could have been much worse. I believe, however, that good will come of it. If you are to be scientists, you must understand that progress is not a straight line. We will go down dead end streets, experiments will fail, and sometimes there will be tragedies. In our attempt to reach the moon equipment failed, rockets caught fire, and men died. We did not stop. Progress demands sacrifice. And sacrifice, by definition, is pain. What we can do is learn from our failures. We can examine the data, determine what went wrong, and do better next time."

Dr. Lehrer began pacing. The class was silent.

"I thought about this a great deal last night. There is talk of ending the Scientopia ani-droid program. I understand the thinking. We welcome the public through our gates every day, and we owe them a safe learning and entertainment experience. But personally, I think it would be a mistake to end the program. We've had years of success, and if we're smart, we will use this experience to create more successes in the future."

Lehrer stopped pacing and looked around the room, pausing for an instant to look at each scholar as he did.

"That's why, until we are ordered to stop, we are going to continue the program. For these last few days we are going to eliminate the classes we had scheduled and work instead on rebuilding Alistair and Dexter. Team Ritchie will work on Dexter while the other three teams will concentrate on Alistair. In recognition of his service and abilities, Max will supervise all four teams, and Hannah will assume his role as leader of Team Ritchie. Good luck."

Max wasn't sure what he was supposed to do as supervisor of all four teams. As Team Ritchie captain, Max only had to work with a few people. Now he had to deal with more than a dozen. Almost immediately he was approached by individuals and small groups who wanted him to settle disagreements. Max was getting his first taste of politics.

Surprisingly, Ryan was very helpful. He organized the group to assemble Alistair's new skeleton, allowing Max to focus on other tasks. Fortunately, Alistair's construction was well-documented and everyone had recent experience. By the end of the first day they had made measurable progress.

Max wasn't too worried about reconstructing Alistair's body. His primary concern was duplicating his programming, the most crucial component of what made Alistair unique. Technicians had recovered the AI chip from the wreckage, but it was one of a kind, and there was a good chance it had been damaged. If it didn't work, Alistair wouldn't be Alistair. He would be unable to think or learn. He would just be another Scientopia ani-droid. Max thought that he might be able to substitute a newer chip that would run the AI module, but that raised a lot of questions. Chip technology had made a lot of progress in the years since Alistair was created. It was possible that a new chip would be even faster and have more power than the original. It was also possible, since the optical AI crystal was an entirely new breed of technology; that a new chip wouldn't work at all.

It was almost time to stop for dinner when Max decided to pay Team Ritchie a visit. They had made visible progress on Dexter. They had taken off the jeans and tee shirt. Although Dexter wasn't anatomically correct, Hannah insisted on covering the sections they weren't working on with a sheet.

"How's it going?" asked Max.

"Maybe another day or two," said Hannah. "We've mostly been replacing broken parts. His circuitry checked out okay. We'll wipe his hard drive and upload the backups tomorrow morning. We may need you for that."

"Okay," said Max. Then, quietly to Hannah, "Wanna go to the Galaxy Grill?"

Hannah looked at him for a time as if considering her answer. "Yes. See you all in the morning."

Max and Hannah walked silently to the lift and started their descent to the atrium.

"You feeling okay today?" Hannah asked Max.

"Feels kind of funny. When it starts hurting, I take a pill. I wouldn't want to go through this again."

"You mean you wouldn't want to save your girlfriend again?"

"My girlfriend?!?"

"You know what I mean. Jumping up on stage in the middle of a performance and attacking a robot you had no way of stopping. You just had to be a hero. It was embarrassing."

"She's just a friend."

"What does that mean? I saw you try to kiss her."

"I would kiss my sister, too; if I had one. And it wouldn't mean anything more."

Hannah smirked and said nothing.

"I think we're going to have a problem restoring Alistair," said Max.

"Trying to change the subject?"

"No, but we've got to get this done. It's important to me. We need to find the Gemini chip. I think it's the only thing that will work. Can you come by tonight and help?"

"You sure know where I am when you need help don't you?"

They got on an APT and rode in silence to the Galaxy Grill stop. As they stepped out of the car Hannah said quietly, "I'll help. But only because of Alistair."

That was good enough for Max.

CHAPTER 23

The receptionist picked up her phone. "Steve, Dr. Lehrer is here to see you."

"Send him in, please."

Sarah smiled at Dr. Lehrer. "He will see you now, Dr. Lehrer."

As Dr. Lehrer walked in, Steve looked up but did not rise from his couch in the sitting area.

"Sit down, Dieter."

Dr. Lehrer took a seat across from Steve.

"Dieter, what are doing? You know about the liability issues. We haven't made any decisions about whether we can continue using ani-droids in the park."

"We are only attempting to rebuild Alistair," said Lehrer. "We must do this to learn what happened."

"Dieter, no one gave you authorization. I'm CEO, and you have to do what I say."

"Don't be ridiculous Steve. You don't know every detail of running the park. Do you dictate the brand of paper towels we use in the restrooms?"

"As a matter of fact, I do."

Dieter couldn't stop himself from rolling his eyes. "Perhaps that's a bad example. The point is, there are many things that go on in the park that escape your attention. You don't have time to do everything. You are the CEO, and I do follow your instructions, which are to explore the technologies important to Scientopia. Ani-droids have long been important to Scientopia, and I think they will continue to be so. The responsible thing is to continue our research to learn what happened."

"I don't think so, Dieter. The lawyers, they're pretty adamant."

"We have visionary lawyers then?"

Steve slapped the table. "Dieter, I have responsibilities. I need you to shut down that program."

"This is a question I want to take up with the board," said Dieter. "In the meantime, the scholars are working on Alistair. It is a good use of their time. We're not taking people away from anything else. Will that be all?"

After two nights in front of their computers, Max and Hannah had searched ten floors of the Crystal Tower with no sign of the Gemini chip. Max was exhausted dreading the thought of getting up in the morning.

"This is too much," said Hannah. "The park is huge. We won't be able to finish a single building before the end of the week. The chip could be anywhere."

"I know," said Max. "I wish there was a way to automate the search." An alert popped on Max's screen. It was from one of his Roblox buddies. He was too tired to play. "Wait a minute! I have an idea. What if we had a bunch of people, hundreds or even thousands to help us search?"

"Where are we going to get hundreds of people to help us search?"

"Roblox."

Hannah wrinkled her forehead. "What do you mean?"

"We create a space on Roblox that is actually the virtual park we see through the emulator. We tell everyone what we're looking for and turn them loose."

"Will that work?"

"They run around looking for Easter eggs, don't they?"

"Yeah, I like doing that," said Hannah.

"See?"

"Why not? What do we need to do?" said Hannah.

Max started formulating a plan to get the emulator running on Roblox. Then he would have to show people what they were looking for and offer a prize for the winner. Max glanced at the clock on his computer screen. It was already past midnight.

"Should we start now?" he asked Hannah.

Hannah sighed. "Probably, we're running out of time."

"You start setting up the space. I'll get some Red Bulls. When I get back, I'll work on integrating the emulator, and you can start recruiting."

It was 3:56 a.m. when Max pushed back from his computer. "I think it's working."

Hannah raised her head off the desk. Even with the Red Bull, she had fallen asleep.

"Already? How did you do it so fast?"

Max smiled. "I'm a genius."

On the morning of the third day after the explosion at the Constellation Theater, Dexter was resurrected. Team Ritchie dressed him in a duplicate of the suit that Alistair wore. The clothes, combined with his intentional resemblance to Alistair, made him look like Alistair Junior.

Sadly, Dexter's appearance was the only thing he shared with the original Alistair. Without an advanced optical chip or AI programming, Dexter would never be able to learn or adapt to situations not anticipated by his programmers.

Their work completed, Team Ritchie joined the other teams to work on Alistair. The combined teams had made progress piecing Alistair together from spare parts. On the outside, he looked complete. It was impossible to tell the new Alistair from the old.

Max gathered the combined teams and their instructors together for the big moment.

"Here goes," Max said. He flipped the switch. All eyes were focused on the reconstructed Alistair. The ani-droid didn't move or speak. It seemed clear that the optical chip had been damaged beyond repair. Alistair was lost to them forever.

Max examined the chip the technicians had extracted from the rebuilt Alistair. It looked intact. The heat from the explosion must have damaged its internal structure. It was worthless. Max dropped it into his pocket.

It was after seven that evening before they were able to login to Roblox. Hannah opened her laptop and started it up. "Heard from Sergey lately?"

Max looked up from his keyboard. "No, and I don't want to."

"Max?"

"What?"

"There are 89 people in our room."

Max looked around. "I only see the two of us."

"In our emulator room on Roblox."

"How can that be? I haven't turned it on yet."

"They're logged in but there's nothing there. Turn it on so they can start."

Max typed at his keyboard. "It's open."

A few minutes later: "Look at this," said Hannah. "We're already up to 127."

Max walked around to Hannah's computer. "How are they finding out about it?"

"I don't know. It must have gotten posted somewhere."

Max heard his instant messenger beep with a new message. He walked around the desk to his computer to see what it was.

"Guy here says he found it."

"Where?"

"Wait a minute…he doesn't know. You know, I didn't think of that. It's not like they can bring the chip to us. Put in the welcome message that people need to take a screenshot and remember what room they're in. I'll tell this guy to see if he can find his way back to where he was."

Within minutes, the screenshots were pouring in, all false alarms. Max had to kick two guys off the server because they were taking screenshots of every room they were in and bringing them to him to check out.

"We could do that ourselves," Max said in an exasperated tone.

"Yeah, pretty ridiculous. Someone here sent a glowing red transformer. How does that look anything like a green crystal? Wait a minute. Max, take a look at this."

Max walked around the desk.

"What?" Max said.

Hannah pointed at her computer. "Here."

Max pushed the screen of Hannah's laptop back to get a better look. It took him a second to realize what he was seeing.

"That's it! I know where it is!"

"Where?"

"Remember the extra star I showed you in the Constellation Theater?"

Hannah shook her head.

"Yeah you do. Right before the performance Kaylee did for us."

"You mean the contest?"

"No, the first one. Just before the lights went down, I showed you the extra star on the ceiling."

"Oh yeah, I remember."

"That's it! The Gemini chip. It's on the ceiling of the Constellation Theater. I wasn't paying that much attention, but it was in the constellation Gemini!"

"We have to get it."

"Now? It's almost 8 o'clock. How will we get in? How will we get up there?"

Max opened a browser to the Scientopia website to check the theater's schedule. "There's a show on now. It'll be over in an hour. We'll go after it closes. I can get in."

"That doesn't tell me how we can get the chip off the ceiling."

Max put his head in his hands. He was too tired to think.

"Max, I'm beat. We've been up late two nights in a row. I hardly got any sleep last night. Let's wait until morning. Maybe we can get Steve or somebody to help us get it down. It's been there for years. It's not going anywhere."

Max struggled to make sense of what she was saying.

"Yeah, you're right. I can't do this. I feel like I'm about to pass out. Message everyone online that the crystal has been found in the theater and the contest is over. Let me know when you send it, and I'll shut the place down."

Max shut down the server and closed his laptop. Hannah rose to leave. Max stood up, stepped to her with open arms and gave her a hug.

"Thanks, Hannah. I couldn't have done it without you."

Hannah smiled. "That's right. Don't forget it. Goodnight, Max."

Max collapsed onto his bed and fell instantly to sleep.

CHAPTER 24

Max woke up early. A faint glow filtered through the blinds but the sun had not yet broken the horizon. He had become accustomed to waking up in Scientopia.

It was difficult not think about the events of the last week. Alistair was gone. The attempted reconstruction and then, last night, locating the Gemini chip. Was it real? Had they really found it? Would today be the day he solved the mystery of Project Gemini? Would the chip give him the power to bring Alistair back? Max's mind was wonderfully clear. After the stress of the explosion, and the days without sleep, he had finally gotten a good night's rest.

A couple of minutes. That's all it took to assure himself that everything was real; that he was not dreaming.

Let's do it, Max thought to himself as he swung out of bed. Standing on the floor he looked down at the clothes he had worn yesterday and then slept in. They were wrinkled, but he had worn worse. Max sniffed under his arm. Not too bad, he thought. No need to change. Max slipped on his shoes, and headed toward Hannah's room, shoelaces flying.

Hannah was already up. "What kept you?" she asked. "I've been waiting for ten minutes."

"I just woke up."

"Never mind. Let's go. I'm so excited. It feels like Christmas morning."

"It does, doesn't it?" said Max.

Outside of the Crystal Tower, the streets of Scientopia were nearly deserted. The park hadn't yet opened, only a few employees were walking about, getting the park ready for a new day of guests.

The APT's weren't running yet, and Max and Hannah were too excited to walk. They broke into a trot making their way through the familiar streets. Max led Hannah through one of his back alley shortcuts that came out only a block away from the theater. Turning onto the street, they passed a man in a knight costume clanking along in the opposite direction. Max half-turned to look at him.

"I didn't know there were knights in Scientopia."

"Scientopia is full of strange things," said Hannah. They could see the theater ahead. "Through the front door or back?" she asked.

Max thought for a second. "The back. Less conspicuous."

As expected, the back door was locked. Max reached for his ID card.

"Let me try," said Hannah.

The indicator on the card reader blinked red.

Max swiped his card. The green light came on, and the door lock clicked. Max smiled triumphantly.

"You just love that, don't you?" asked Hannah.

"What's not to like?"

Hannah groaned. "Yeah? Well, that's not going to help you get the chip down from the ceiling. Have a plan yet?"

"I'm not worried about it," said Max.

They entered the theater, moved down the corridor, and through the double door at the back of the stage.

"Hey, it's dark in here, where are the lights?"

"I'll get 'em. Hold the door open so I can see." Max felt his way over to the electrical panel and pulled the big lever for the house lights. There was a clunk as the lights came on and started to buzz. They walked to the front of the stage, Max keeping his eyes up, searching the ceiling as he went.

"I don't see it," Max said. "I think another switch must make the stars come on."

"Max, look!" Hannah was pointing out into the auditorium.

"What?"

"In the aisle. What's that?"

Max saw what Hannah saw. It was a scissor lift. Max looked up. It was directly below the Gemini constellation. "The chip's gone!" Max looked back down at the lift. "Someone took it."

Max and Hannah looked at each other. "Crap," said Max. "It was the knight. That was Sergey."

"How did he know?"

"He must have been tracking us online. We've got to stop him before he gets out of the park."

"What are you going to do, Max? He's a grown man; you're just a kid. You can't stop him."

Max's mind was racing. "I have an idea, but we have to hurry."

Max bolted from the theater without another word. Hannah did her best to keep up.

"Where are we going, Max?"

"To the Crystal Tower. I need the VR helmet."

"In Steve's office? People are there now. How are you going to get in? What are you going to do with it?"

"I don't know yet," said Max without slowing down. "Go to the lab and turn on Dexter. Take him to the courtyard and wait."

Hannah was out of breath. She grunted agreement.

Max and Hannah separated in the atrium. He took the lift to Steve's office, she the one to the Death Star and the lab where Dexter was stored. On the ride up Max was trying to anticipate what he might find in Steve's office. He thought of what he might say if questioned by a security guard or Sarah the receptionist and hoped Steve wasn't there.

When the elevator doors opened, Max bolted down the hall to the glass doors of Steve's office. Max saw that Sarah was already at her desk. He punched in the access code and pushed the door open.

Sarah tried to hide her surprise and said, "Good morning, Max. I wasn't expecting you. What can I do for you?"

Max didn't slow down enough to reply. By the time Sarah had finished her greeting, Max had shot past the desk. Over his shoulder, he yelled, "I need the VR helmet."

Max rocketed into Steve's office and turned towards the loft.

Steve was at this desk. "Max, what are you doing?"

"I need the helmet!"

"Why?"

Max paused. It only took a second for him to decide that the truth was his best bet. Trying to catch his breath he sputtered, "The Gemini chip. We found it. Sergey has it. We have to stop him. He's getting away."

Steve's eye's widened, but otherwise he appeared to remain calm. "Slow down, Max. Where is Sergey now?"

"He's in the park somewhere. I need the helmet to find him."

"And you say he has the Gemini chip?"

Max nodded vigorously.

"It's no problem, Max. I'm glad you came to me."

Steve picked up the smartphone on his desk. He put the phone on speaker and dialed a four-digit number.

"Scientopia Security."

"It's Steve, let me speak to the head of security, please."

"This is Mark," said another voice.

"Good morning, Mark. We have a problem. Sergey Mamontov is in the park, and we need to apprehend him. I want you to put the park on Level-5 lockdown. No one is to come or go until we find him. Just a second. Max, what is Sergey wearing?"

"Armor."

"Armor?"

"You know, shiny metal, like a knight wears."

Steve smiled. "Did you hear that, Mark? Sergey was last seen wearing armor. Let me know when you find him."

"Will do," said Mark.

Steve ended the connection and walked towards Max. "Come here Max, let's sit down, and you tell me what's going on."

Max told Steve how they had located the Gemini chip and how Sergey must have been tracking them and beat them to it.

"That sounds like Sergey," said Steve. "I have to tell you that it has been a disappointment how you have maintained contact after I warned you about him."

Max looked surprised.

"Yes, I know. I also know you were here in the office using the helmet a couple of weeks ago. Was that something Sergey told you to do?"

Max lowered his eyes.

"Why have you kept talking to Sergey? What has he been telling you?"

"He said he would tell me more about my mom and why she was on that plane."

Steve ran his hand through his hair. "Oh, Max. I understand. What a terrible thing to for him to say. At one time, I would have done anything to find out about my birth mother, too."

Steve took a seat next to Max.

"Max look at me. Your mother was a fine woman. I wish she were here today. She would be very proud of you. The truth is she got on an airplane heading back from Florida. Some of our employees were also aboard for company business. The plane went down in the Gulf of Mexico with everyone on board. There is no mystery. It was a sad day for everyone here at Scientopia."

Steve put his hand on Max's shoulder. "Do you understand?"

A tear ran down Max's cheek. He looked away to tried to regain his composure.

"What else did Sergey tell you?"

"That Project Gemini is too important for one company. He said it should belong to everyone."

"Do you believe that's what he wants?"

"No. I think he wants to use it to come back to Scientopia. I think he wants to be in charge."

"I think you're right, Max."

Steve and Max remained on the couch talking for what seemed to Max a long time. He texted Hannah that it was taking longer than he thought. The longer he sat, the more he became convinced that Sergey was going to get away with the chip, dashing his hopes of rebuilding Alistair.

Finally, Max spoke up. "Please, can't I try the helmet? He's going to get away."

"Max, it would be impossible for anyone to get in or out of the park. We're on total lockdown."

"You don't know him. He's into the computer system. He has all of these disguises. He's so sneaky."

"What do you think you can do with the helmet, Max?"

"I think I can find him."

"How would you be able to find him if Security can't, Max? They have access to the same information you do."

Max pulled out his smartphone in frustration. He noticed that Hannah hadn't texted him back. He sent another message: *where r u?*

"Not exactly," Max said to Steve. "Security doesn't have access to the same information I do. You can't track Sergey on your network can you?"

Steve's expression answered the question. "You can?" Steve asked.

Max shrugged.

"Well, can you?"

"I think so."

"Why didn't you tell me?"

"You didn't ask."

Steve picked up his phone. "Sarah, will you get Greg Symonds in here pronto?"

Max had pulled his phone out again and saw that Hannah still hadn't responded. When he looked up he saw that Steve was looking at him curiously.

"All right, Max. Let's give it a try."

They climbed to the loft and started the computer. Max plugged the emulator into the USB port just as Greg arrived.

"It's an emulator. It turns all of the parks electronics and information into a virtual world that you can navigate. It's how we found the chip."

Max pulled up a screen showing the places he could go to in the park.

"What do you think of this, Greg?" Steve asked.

"It's amazing. How did you do this?" said Greg.

"Sergey did it. He gave me the drive."

"Does this mean you don't need the helmet?" asked Greg.

"You can do some of the stuff the helmet does. But you can see more with the helmet, and it's a much faster connection. I need the helmet now to locate Sergey."

Steve looked from the computer screen to Greg. "Do you see any problem with him using the helmet?"

Greg shook his head. "Hard to say. There is the possibility that Sergey could do something to start a feedback loop. It would overload Max like before. We would see it on the graph here," said Greg pointing to a graph on the screen.

"If there was a problem could you disconnect him in time?" asked Steve.

"I think so."

Steve looked at Max. "You heard him. Are you up for it?"

Max stood up and reached for the helmet. "Yeah, I can do it."

When he put the helmet on, Max's mind flashed white while it made the connection. When the image popped into his mind Max was just where he wanted to be: outside on the plaza at the entrance to the Crystal Tower. Neither Hannah nor Dexter was anywhere to be seen. Using the security cameras, Max swept around the other sides of the building as well.

"I don't see Hannah or Dexter," Max said to Steve. "They were supposed to be waiting for me outside. She's not answering texts either. They're gone!"

CHAPTER 25

Max paused to consider how he could find Hannah and Dexter. He accessed Hannah's security card logs. The card hadn't been swiped since she left the Crystal Tower ten minutes before. Dexter hadn't been logged into any checkpoints either.

"Is the park's facial recognition working?" asked Max.

Greg looked at Steve. Steve nodded.

"Yes," said Greg.

"Where is it?"

"On the security network. But it won't help find Sergey if he is in disguise."

"Yes, but it can find Hannah."

"That could take a couple of hours," said Greg.

"Not if I limit the search to only people in the park. There's hardly anyone here now." Max accessed Hannah's park ID photo and had the system run a search. Two long minutes later the system pulled a live camera feed.

"Are you seeing this on the screen?" Max asked.

"We are."

Max saw three figures. There was Sergey, still in the knight costume, and Dexter. Dexter was holding Hannah by the wrist, pulling her along.

"What's Dexter doing?" asked Steve.

"He's following Sergey's orders," replied Max.

"Where are they?" asked Greg.

Max quickly checked his map. "They're in the compound. There's an unattended gatehouse nearby. He must be trying to get out through it."

"Flip to the next camera, Max."

Max went to the next security camera. Sergey and Dexter were running, Hannah stumbling along still in Dexter's grip. They were heading right for the gatehouse.

There was a short arched tunnel right through the middle of the gatehouse with an aluminum gate at either end.

"What's in the gatehouse?" Max asked Steve.

"Nothing. It hasn't been used for years. It's supposed to be locked."

"The lock won't stop him. I'll see if I can," said Max. "Tell the security teams. We may be able to trap him."

"Security, this is Steve. Sergey is at gate fourteen. Send a team there immediately."

Max let Sergey through the inner gate. When the inner gate swung closed, Max closed the lock. When the lock clicked Max saw Sergey on the security camera look back at the gate suspiciously. But he didn't stop. He stepped quickly towards the outer gate. Max entered an override code into the lock's electronic control panel to keep it from opening. Nothing happened. The security camera didn't cover the center of the gatehouse tunnel, and Max couldn't tell what was going on.

"I think they're trapped in the tunnel between the inner and outer gates," said Max. "But I can't see anything."

"We have him," said Steve. "Security will be there in less than a minute."

When it seemed to Max like he could run there faster himself, the four-man security team appeared on camera. The security team hesitated a moment and then moved in, out of the camera's view.

After a few seconds, Steve's phone buzzed. "They say there's no one there."

"Where did they go?" asked Max.

"There's an entrance to the tunnel system there. It was supposed to be chained close."

"Okay, I'll take a look."

Max used the emulator to scan the tunnels. There was nothing but some stairs down to an empty hallway. "I can't see much," said Max. "Where are the cameras?"

"There aren't any," said Steve. "That's an old area so we didn't put the security upgrades there. Don't worry; the security team is searching the tunnels now."

Several tense minutes passed as they waited to hear from the security team. When Steve's phone buzzed again, his side of the conversation told the whole story. "Where could they have gone?"

Max took off the helmet. "The helmet is no good down there. Can you take me to the tunnels?"

Steve and Greg reluctantly agreed. As they exited the Crystal Tower Steve led them to his personal golf cart. The trio sped through the nearly empty streets of Scientopia toward Gate 14.

"This is killing us," said Steve. "We're losing $200,000 every hour we delay opening."

Steve brought the cart to a hard stop outside the gatehouse and led the way down into the catacombs. Before Max's eyes could adjust to the dim light, he was assaulted by a musty smell. Max could feel the dampness coming from the bare concrete walls. Lighting was provided by fluorescent fixtures hanging from overhead pipes.

"How far does this go?" asked Max.

"They run all over the park," said Steve. "But this section is supposed to be sealed off. No one but security should have been down here for the last ten years."

The security team leader came up to Steve to give a report. While Steve and Greg were distracted by the security team's report Max moved down the tunnel.

"Don't go too far, Max," said Steve. "We don't want to lose you, too."

That sounded to Max like permission to proceed. He started to explore the corridors running off of the main tunnel. Some had doors, all locked with old manual locks that took a key to open. Unless Sergey had a key, which was possible, he hadn't used them.

The only door that didn't fit the pattern was a solid wood door next to a metal-framed, black window. Max leaned closer to the glass to see if he could make out what was in the room. As he moved closer, he realized that the glass has been painted black from the inside. Max turned his attention to the security keypad mounted on the wall next to the door. This was the only door with an electronic lock.

Steve and Greg were still discussing the situation with the security team. They weren't paying any attention to Max. He punched **23564** into the keypad and heard the *click* of the lock disengaging. Max turned the knob and froze when he heard Steve's voice.

"There's nothing in there, Max," yelled Steve. "It's just an old security station."

The door was already open, and Max wanted to take a look. He couldn't see a thing except darkness. Max reached inside, searching for a light switch but couldn't find one. He took a couple of steps forward into the dark and bumped into a swivel chair and a desk. His left foot collided with something metal. He fumbled in the darkness and realized it was a storage cabinet.

"Max," called Greg from down the hall. "Come on, we need to get going."

Max turned to rejoin the adults when he noticed an extremely faint glow on the floor near the storage cabinet. Using the barely perceptible light as a guide, he felt his way along the wall and found a doorknob. He turned the knob. It rotated about a quarter turn and then stopped. Max braced his shoulder against the door and pushed as hard as he could. To his surprise, it swung inward revealing another tunnel. This new tunnel was dimly lit but he could see an open door at the other end.

"Max? What are you doing in there?" Greg's voice was coming closer.

"Just a second," Max yelled back. "There's a light on in here."

Without warning, someone struck Max from behind knocking him to the floor. He heard a door slam, followed by the sound of a dead bolt sliding home.

"Good boy, Max. I didn't think it would take you long to find me."

It was Sergey. Sergey grabbed him by the collar and dragged him towards the open door at the end of the tunnel.

"What are you doing?" said Max. "You can't get away, they're right behind me. Steve and the security team will be here in seconds."

As soon as he said it, Max heard banging and voices from the far side of the door that Sergey had locked behind them.

"That door is two inches of solid steel. They'll have to cut it down. It will take hours. We'll be gone long before that."

"You're locked in, too," said Max.

Sergey laughed. "There are a dozen ways out of here Max, and I know them better than anyone."

They reached the door at the end of the tunnel. Sergey pulled Max into a large room. Max felt an unfamiliar tingling at the back of his neck. The chamber was as gloomy as the rest of the catacombs and dirtier. It looked like a lab, but the equipment was ancient. There were single piece monitors and keyboards, a clunky computer tower that came nearly to his waist, even a rack of computer storage tapes. Only a few lights near the door were on, the rest of the room stretched away to dim shapes. At the far edge of the darkness, Max saw a familiar form. It was Dexter. He was holding Hannah.

"Hannah!"

"Max?!?"

"Yeah, are you okay?"

"Yes, but he's holding me so tight. My arm hurts."

Max looked at Sergey. "What are you going to do?"

"Don't be so dramatic, Max. I don't plan on hurting anyone unless I have to. I only want what's mine. I'll take the chip," Sergey held up a bag that was hanging at his side, "and leave you and your little girlfriend to enjoy the rest of your stay at Scientopia. It wasn't my plan to involve anyone else. But I saw her and your dumb anidroid friend, and they seemed like the insurance I needed to get out of the park."

Sergey lowered the bag. "Before we leave, I want to show you something." Sergey turned to his right and flipped the light switches next to the door frame. Suddenly the room was bathed in fluorescent light.

"What do you think of your father's lab?"

"What do you mean?"

"Then you don't know yet, do you? Of course, Steve hasn't told you, why would he? You're nothing but a threat to him."

"I don't know what you're talking about." Max winced as the buzzing in his head grew louder.

"Don't you, Max? Has it never occurred to you that all of the things you can do are not by chance? That there is an explanation?"

"Maybe."

"Everything happens for a reason, Max. Your biological father is the great Verner Hoff. You are not Max Powers, you are Maximilian Hoff."

"You're lying. How would you know that?"

"Our friend Steve somehow got a sample of your DNA and compared it to Hoff's. There is no doubt."

Max heard what Sergey was saying, but he couldn't think about it. His mind was focused only on how to get the chip and then get away from Sergey. He didn't think Sergey planned to hurt them, but he couldn't be sure.

Suddenly Max remembered the odd tingling sensation he felt when Sergey dragged him into the room. It reminded him of the feeling he experienced when he was using the VR helmet. Did the tingling mean he was somehow connected to the network now? He usually interacted with the network while his eyes were closed. Closing his eyes now would surely tip off Sergey. He had to access the network without closing his eyes or making Sergey suspicious.

Dexter! Max thought as loud as he could. Nothing. He tried again. *Hello, Dexter.*

Instantly, there was a reply. *Hello, Max.*

Max's heart jumped. He heard Dexter, but he wasn't sure if Dexter had used his vocalizer or if it had come across the network. Max studied Sergey for any sign that he had heard the ani-droid speak. After a few moments, it became clear to Max that he was communicating with Dexter through the wireless network.

Whatever he did he had to do it *now*. Sergey was still talking about Verner Hoff. Max tried to pretend he was listening while he formulated a plan.

Getting away was the priority, but he should try to grab the chip if he could.

Dexter was the problem and the solution. Hannah was his prisoner and Max didn't know if he could order the ani-droid to release her. What if Sergey had tampered with his programming? If Max could regain control of Dexter, he could order him to restrain Sergey. Whatever he did, there would be no second chances.

"...what do you think of that, Max?" Sergey asked.

Max froze. He hadn't heard Sergey's question. He decided to ignore it.

"Where are you taking us?"

"Don't worry, if you cooperate you won't be harmed," said Sergey.

"Why don't you take the chip and leave us here? You'll have everything you want."

"I can't do that, Max. I need you, or at least one of you, as insurance if I'm stopped. Now that you mention it, I don't need both of you. It would be much easier with only one. Fewer chances for something to go wrong. Hannah has been a good companion so far. I'll take her. You, young Mr. Hoff, will remain here. Now I need something to tie you up before we leave."

Sergey began searching drawers and cabinets.

"Computer tape, that should work."

It was time for Max to act. He closed his eyes and sent: *Dexter, release Hannah.*

Max opened his eyes and saw Dexter releasing his grip on Hannah. Max's gaze shifted back to Sergey. He was trying to unwind the computer tape from its spindle and hadn't noticed Dexter's movement.

Now for the next step. Max closed his eyes again sent the next command. *Dexter, get Sergey's bag.* Max opened his eyes. Dexter was moving his head. Max had never really noticed the sounds that Dexter made before, but in the quiet of the underground lab, the whirring of the servo motor that turned Dexter's head was very loud.

Sergey looked up. Surprise filled his face.

There was no time for subtlety. "Dexter, hold Sergey!" screamed Max. That should have been his first command. When Dexter grabbed Sergey, getting the chip would be no problem.

"Stop, Dexter!" shouted Sergey.

Dexter took another step and stopped.

"Dexter, hold Sergey!" Dexter moved forward again.

Before Sergey could speak again, Hannah saw her opportunity and lunged straight at him. He stepped back in surprise and threw up his arms to cover his face as she attacked.

Before Sergey could react, Hannah grabbed the bag out of Sergey's left hand. Sergey staggered forward to retrieve it but lost his balance and fell to the floor. As he fell, he grabbed Hannah's ankle, causing her to tumble backward.

"Max!" screamed Hannah. She tossed the bag to Max. He caught it, reached in, grabbed the chip and slipped it into his pocket.

"Dexter, hold Sergey!" yelled Max.

Dexter lumbered towards Sergey. Sergey stood up and pulled Hannah towards him. "Dexter, shut down," said Sergey.

"Dexter, hold Sergey!" Max yelled again. Nothing happened. "Dexter, answer." Still nothing happened. Max closed his eyes to try and reach Dexter directly. There was no response.

Sergey was now standing with his arm around Hannah's neck. "Good try, Max. There's nothing more you can do, which leaves us with a problem. I have something you want and you have something I want. Why don't we trade?"

Hannah shook her head.

Sergey laughed. "Max, your girlfriend is trying to be brave. I don't think she has considered the consequences of a standoff. She is the one with the most to lose."

"You can't get out of here," said Max. "The tunnel is full of security and there's more on the way."

"Then what do you have to lose, Max? You'll get it back in a few minutes after they catch me. Right?"

Max reluctantly took the chip out of his pocket and looked at it.

"Don't, Max," said Hannah. "He won't hurt me."

"Let her go first," said Max.

"You bring me the chip, and I'll let her go when you hand it to me."

Max held out his hand with the chip and moved cautiously towards Sergey. When he was about three feet away Sergey's arm darted out and grabbed the chip. At the same time, he released Hannah. Max took Hannah's hand and pulled her toward him, away from Sergey.

"You're a smart boy, Max. Like your father. Your real father. You should be flattered, Hannah. Max must like you a lot."

Sergey ran for the door. "See you on Roblox, Max." He disappeared down the hall with the optical chip grasped firmly in his hand.

"Max, I can't believe you did that for me. I know how much you wanted the chip. How are we going to get it back?"

Max shrugged. "Don't worry about it. At least you're safe."

"Let's get out of here. We need to tell them that Sergey escaped."

Max took out his phone. "I'll text Steve."

Fifteen minutes later security found another way in. Steve, Greg, and a large group of security officers hurried into the lab. "Which way did he go?" one of the security guards asked. Max pointed down the hall, and four security officers took off in pursuit.

"Are you two okay?" Steve asked.

"We're fine," said Hannah. "Max saved us."

"He's making a habit of that," said Steve. "Sergey got the chip?"

Max smiled and put his hand into his pocket. "He got a chip." Max pulled something from his pocket and held it out to Steve. "But he didn't get *the* chip."

"What?!?" Steve exclaimed.

Hannah punched Max's shoulder. "Why didn't you tell me?"

Max smiled at Steve. "I gave him the broken chip that we salvaged from Alistair." Max laughed as he turned to Hannah.

"I didn't want to say anything because I was afraid Sergey might come back, and I didn't want you to know."

"I need you working for me. You're a sharp kid, Max," said Steve.

Steve's comment brought a flood of recent memories back to Max; ones that he had been too busy to process when he heard them. The smile left Max's face.

"Steve, there's something I want to ask you about. Things that Sergey was telling me."

Steve bit his lip and held up his hand. "Wait a second," said Steve. He took a long breath. "It's about your father isn't it, Max?"

"Yes, he said…"

Steve interrupted: "He said that Verner Hoff is your father?"

"Yes."

"It's true, Max. I ran the DNA; it's a match. I've been waiting for a good time to tell you and your father together. There are a lot of things to work out, and I didn't want to break the news until we had some answers."

Max dropped his head.

Steve put his finger on Max's chin and gently raised it up. "It's a good thing, Max. You have opportunities now that you wouldn't have dreamed of yesterday. But it's going to take some getting used to. Your world is going to change, and it's not just the money. People are going to treat you differently. They're going to want things from you. You're not going to know whom to trust. It's going to be a big adjustment for you and your father. Speaking of your father. Do you want me to tell him or do you want to?"

Max shook the thoughts from his head. "I'll tell him. But could you be there when I do?"

Steve pulled Max close for a hug. "Sure, Max. I'll always be here for you."

Max pulled away and took a deep breath. There were so many question he had, but there was one thing he knew he needed to answer. Max examined the chip in his hand. "Can I go put the chip in Alistair? We need to bring him back."

Steve took the chip from Max and looked at it. "I don't see why not. Be sure and have Greg and Dieter help you. We don't want to risk this thing."

Max looked at Greg with pleading eyes.

"OK, Max, let's get going," said Greg.

"I'll meet you there. Come on, Hannah, let's go."

Max ran most of the way to the Crystal Tower. It might have been faster to take an APT, but Max was too impatient to go through the station. There was another reason too. Sitting in an APT car would have given Hannah the opportunity to ask more questions. Having to run at least slowed her probing, though not by much.

"Max, I didn't know you were adopted. Why didn't you tell me? Did you have any idea you were Hoff's son? Do you know how amazing that is? You can come here anytime and do anything, all for free! It's so awesome. Max, are you listening to me?"

"I don't know what it means yet. We can talk about it later. Hurry, I can't wait to get Alistair working again."

Max and Hannah bolted through the atrium. Steve hadn't wasted any time in opening the gates, and guests were wandering in. The Death Star was displaying a 360-degree fireworks show.

As they exited the lift, Max asked Hannah to find Dr. Lehrer while he began working on Alistair. Max entered the lab and turned on the lights. It seemed like days had passed since they realized Sergey had beaten them to the chip. It was still early, however, and the lab was empty. Max remembered that it was the last day of the Summer Genius program, and they were on a delayed schedule. Max was glad that he would have a chance to restore Alistair without distractions.

It was disturbing to see his friend inert on the lab table, a collection of inanimate metal and plastic. Max looked more closely at the chip. Max hoped this piece of crystal would give back to Alistair what he had lost.

Max removed Alistair's chest panel. He carefully extracted the processor board. Max examined the wires connected to the board. Max moved the board aside, being careful not to put any stress on the wires. Max now had a clear view of the recessed slot designed to hold the AI chip. Max held the chip just above the connecting pins, checking the fit.

"Careful, Max. Please, wait a moment."

Max turned and saw Dr. Lehrer, Greg and Hannah entering the lab.

"I'm just checking the fit of the new chip, Dr. Lehrer."

"I know you are eager to restore Alistair, Max. But first things first. We should run some diagnostics on the chip to make sure it's compatible. We would look very foolish plugging it in and burning it out when we flipped the switch. Agreed?"

"Yes, sir," said Max.

"Good. Dr. Symonds, will you show Max how to go through the testing routines? I have some work to do. I'll be back in about an hour to see what you've found."

Max and Hannah followed Greg to the test bench. They stood by while Greg started up the equipment and plugged in the chip. With both Alistair and the chip being nonstandard, nothing could be taken for granted.

After a full hour had passed, Greg announced that the chip and Alistair were a perfect match.

When Dr. Lehrer returned, he insisted on questioning Greg in minute detail about the test results. It took another half hour of discussion before Lehrer was satisfied.

Greg handed the chip to Max. "Will you do the honors?"

After all they had been through to locate and secure it, installing the chip was anticlimactic. Max centered the pins over the slots and pushed. That was it. A two-second job.

"Power him up?" Max asked.

"Let's put everything back and button him up first," said Dr. Lehrer.

Max replaced the processor board and returned Alistair's chest plate to its proper position.

"Now?" asked Max.

"Go ahead."

Max plugged in Alistair's external power cable. He opened a small access door in the side of Alistair's chest. Alistair was the most advanced ani-droid in the world, but his on/off switch was old school. It was a simple metal toggle switch like hobbyists used to buy at Radio Shack. Max put his finger on the switch. He paused, closed his eyes and thought, *Please work*. He flipped the switch.

Nothing. Max flipped the switch off and back on again. Still nothing.

"Wait a second and see if he warms up," said Greg.

A long minute later and Alistair remained still.

"Hey," said Hannah. "Do you need to give him an activation code, like when you started his AI?"

Max lit up. "Maybe so!" Max thought about it for a few seconds, but nothing came to him. *Wait*, thought Max.

Max suddenly blurted out "**36850**." A small red LED next to the switch flashed three times and then went dark. He repeated the code multiple times without success.

Dr. Lehrer put his hand on Max's shoulder. "Don't be discouraged, Max. Science is never a straight line. We'll keep working and see if we can bring him back."

CHAPTER 26

The remainder of that day, his last day as a Summer Genius, was a miserable blur. The rest of the Summer Geniuses eventually arrived. Adults and Summer Geniuses tried test after test in an attempt to revive Alistair. By late morning, the other teams had drifted away to pack and prepare for departure. Team Ritchie members stayed with Max a little longer but they also had to get ready to leave.

Max was out of ideas, but he still couldn't tear himself away from the lab table. He stood vigil over Alistair until Dr. Lehrer told him he had to attend the final assembly at 3:00.

Adults gave speeches and handed out certificates and awards. Max saw his dad in the audience. He didn't remember much else. As they were being dismissed, a messenger approached him and said his dad would meet him in Steve's office.

They went. Max didn't feel like talking, so Steve delivered the news of Max's supposed father. Hearing it again he still didn't believe it. He didn't even want it to be true. Science could say what it would, but it couldn't turn Verner Hoff, a man he had never met, into his father. Tim Powers was Max's father, and all of the DNA tests in the world wouldn't change that.

Despite his gloom, Max did rouse himself in an effort to comfort his father. Max could tell it was a shock to him. "Are you sure? What does this mean?" he had said.

"Dad, this doesn't change anything. I just want to go home and get back to school."

Max couldn't believe he heard himself saying that. Max was good at school, he liked school, but he was not one of those crazy kids who hungered to get back to it.

There were too many other things to do to be wishing for more school. Roblox for example. Max decided that he must be feeling bad if he was hoping to get back to school.

"Ready to go home, son?" Max's dad asked as they left Steve's office.

"Can we stop by and see about Alistair? To say goodbye."

"Sure."

When Max and his dad entered the lab, Dr. Lehrer, Greg, and a couple of technicians were discussing the attempts to revive Alistair.

"Good, Max, you are here. Come talk to us," said Dr. Lehrer. "I'm afraid the news is not good. We have concluded that the chip is empty. Apparently, it was never loaded with the same AI matrix as the original or it has been damaged. Perhaps Project Gemini failed, and they were unable to develop or install the matrix. We do not know."

"So, this is it?" asked Max.

Lehrer looked at Max sympathetically. "We can work on it one more day, but we do not have the resources to continue past that."

Max tried to contain the despair that suddenly overwhelmed him.

"Do not be sad, Max. Alistair was a very good experiment. We learned much from him. I think we will be able to create a better class of ani-droids because of Alistair. I hope you will help us do that."

His dad's hand rested lightly on his shoulder.

"Thank you, Dr. Lehrer, for everything you've done for Max this summer. We're grateful."

Max barely managed to hold back tears. "Thank you, Dr. Lehrer, Greg. I had a great time and learned a lot."

"You are welcome Max. We'll let you know if we make any progress."

On the way home, his father stopped for frozen yogurt. It was a familiar ritual, something they had done many times. It helped Max begin the transition back to the life he had left several weeks ago. He wanted things to get back to normal as soon as possible.

"How was school?" his father asked when Max came in the front door.

"It was good. What are you doing home?"

"I wanted to see how your first day went. You're growing up so fast. You're not going to be my little Max for much longer." His father hugged him. "I'm going back to work for a couple of hours. I thought we could have pizza tonight. How does that sound?"

"Pepperoni and sausage?"

"You bet," said Mr. Powers.

"Sounds good, Dad. See you later."

Max plopped onto his bed. It was the first day of school, so he didn't have any real homework. Out of the corner of his eye he saw his Scientopia backpack. It had lain there unopened since he returned from the park.

Might as well get it over with, thought Max. He rose from the bed and opened the bag. He tossed a few shirts into the dirty clothes bin. He pulled out a plastic necklace he'd won tossing rings onto cones. There was his Summer Genius Program completion certificate, a little wrinkled, but worth keeping. He spread it smooth and put it loosely in a photo album for safe keeping. Finally, as Max fished around in the bottom for any small thing he'd missed, he felt a thin metallic object. It was Alistair's disc-shaped nameplate.

Max rolled the nameplate between his fingers, studied it a moment, and tossed it in his desk drawer. As he moved to close the drawer he caught a glimpse of the medallion his mother had given him years ago and froze.

Before this moment, he hadn't realized how similar they were. His medallion had been hanging around his neck so long he'd almost forgotten what it looked like.

Max picked them up and compared them. It took only a second to realize that they were virtually identical. Same size, same color, same weight, same typeface. One said *Max* the other *Alistair*. Max flipped both discs over. He stared at them, confused. He had never paid attention to the indentions on the back of his medallion. He had thought that similar indentions on Alistair's nameplate were from the explosion. Looking closely, he saw they weren't in the same pattern but were otherwise too similar for them to be there by chance.

Max held the discs up side by side. Something was familiar about the patterns, but Max couldn't place them. He sat on his bed, then laid back, lost in thought. Looking up at the stars painted on his ceiling he felt a shiver run up his spine. *That was it!* Without a question. The back of each disk represented one half of the constellation Gemini. Alistair's had the star Castor on his, and Max's had Pollux. The Twins. They were a matched pair. This was not an accident. It was a deliberate message that he and Alistair were linked, on purpose, by Project Gemini.

Max ran to his father.

"Wait a minute," said Mr. Powers as he was washing the grease off his hands. "Why do we need to go to Scientopia right away?"

"It's the medallion mom gave me before she died," said Max. "It's the same as what was inside Alistair. Except his has one of the Gemini stars and mine has the other."

"I still don't see why we need to go right now."

"Alistair's medallion is linked to his prototype chip. Mine must be linked to the newer chip. This might be the key to reviving Alistair."

Mr. Powers frowned at the thought of going back to Scientopia.

"Let me see Alistair's medallion," he said as he finished drying his hands. Mr. Powers studied the disk. "I don't see how this would work. There's nothing for it to plug into."

Mr. Powers studied the medallion for a few more seconds before shaking his head.

"I don't see the harm in trying. Tomorrow. I just finished working, and Scientopia is too far to drive this late in the day. We'll go first thing after school."

Max looked deflated. His father walked over and put his hand on Max's shoulder to comfort him. "I know you feel like Alistair is your long lost brother, but he can wait another day. He's not going anywhere."

"OK, but can we go first thing tomorrow?"

"First thing after school. You may be Alistair's brother, but you can't just download your knowledge like he does. You still have to do it the old fashioned way." Mr. Powers grinned. "One day at a time. Just like the rest of us. Anyway, tickets are a lot cheaper in the evening."

"Dad! I don't need tickets anymore," reminded Max. "I can go, we can go, anytime we like now!"

"I forgot, you're Maximillian Hoff now!" joked his father.

"Dad!" Max rolled his eyes. "I will always be Max Powers."

The drive to Scientopia seemed to take longer than usual due to Max's growing anticipation. At first, he was annoyed that Hannah had insisted on coming along, but now he was glad she was with him.

Steve and Greg greeted them when they arrived, tipped off by the code Max had typed into the gate at employee parking. Max explained his theory to Steve and Greg as they raced to the lab.

"It was hidden in Alistair," sputtered Max. "We didn't find it until he, uh, died."

Dr. Lehrer looked at the medallion and then back at Max. "Ani-droids don't die. They just...stop."

"Can't we at least try?" pleaded Hannah. "We came all this way."

"I never said you couldn't try," he replied. "I just hope it's worth the effort."

Dr. Lehrer handed the medallion back to Max. Max walked over to Alistair's lifeless form and studied it. He had no idea what to do next.

"Put it near the chip," said Hannah.

Max shrugged, and placed the medallion on Alistair's chest approximately where the chip was mounted.

"Now what?" asked Steve.

"The passcode!" said Max. "Let's see, **36850**." The red light flashed and went dead, just like last time. Max repeated the code, as if it were an incantation. Nothing happened.

Mr. Powers put his hand on Max's shoulder. "It's okay, son. It was a long shot."

Max didn't understand. He *knew* the medallion was the key.

"Maximillian?" asked Dr. Lehrer. "Could there be a different passcode for this chip?"

"I don't know," Max replied.

"The passcode you're using might only be for Alistair's old chip." Dr. Lehrer said. "That was the alpha Gemini chip, not this beta chip."

"Wait a second," exclaimed Hannah.

All eyes turned to Hannah. "Did you say the chip was beta Gemini? Like beta Geminorum?"

"That's right," said Max. "Sergey said those were the chips' names. Alpha Geminorum and Beta Geminorum."

"Max, don't you see? Those are the names of the twin stars in Gemini. Castor and Pollux!"

"And my medallion has the star Pollux on it and Alistair's had Castor," said Max excitedly.

"So," said Steve stroking his chin, "the passcode has something to do with those stars?"

Before he could finish his sentence, Hannah had her phone out, searching online.

"Max, what was that number again?"

"36850."

Hannah typed the number into her search and squealed. "It's here!"

"What?" cried Max.

"The number is Castor's HIP number. That's its *Hipparcos Catalogue* number."

Max looked at her confused.

"It's a way to catalogue all the stars, and here's the HIP number for Pollux."

Hannah handed her phone to Max. Max slowly walked over to Alistair and took a deep breath. He flipped on Alistair's switch and waited for a few seconds. He didn't know why, but he wanted to make sure he wasn't rushing.

"**37826**," said Max.

The light flashed red three times and went dark. Everyone sighed in disappointment. Then it turned green. Slowly, Alistair's eyes opened.

Alistair sat up ramrod straight, staring straight ahead with no expression on his face. In a cold, mechanical voice, he said, "Beta Geminorum installation complete." Then the ani-droid froze and went silent.

Max walked up and looked into Alistair's eyes, which stared straight ahead. Max frowned. Perhaps the new chip wasn't compatible with Alistair and his memories and personality were truly gone.

"Ani-droid Alistair system check complete."

Alistair turned his head toward Max. Slowly a grin spread across Alistair's face. "Max, I'm glad to see you survived my explosive personality. Are you doing okay? I'd be upset if you were hurt."

Max smiled. "Upset? I know how to fix that! Would you like a Hoffpop? They come in seven fruity flavors."

-end-

Keith Philips

Made in the USA
San Bernardino, CA
10 April 2017